To Testify from the Grave Book Two

Richard Anthony Sattanni

America Star Books
Frederick, Maryland

Softcover 9781682292471
PUBLISHED BY AMERICA STAR BOOKS, LLLP
www. americastarbooks. pub
Frederick, Maryland

First a special thank you to my wife MIRIAM for her understanding as I worked on this murder mystery.

Another thank you to my most loved AUNT NELLIE who believed I had talent to become a writer. Thank you so much.

Another special person I need to give a special thank you is JOHN CALABRO a life long friend who takes care of my website.

These are the other books by the author—
1. THE SIR DAVID THOMAS SERIES—
2. TO TESTIFY FROM THE GRAVE
3. THE LAURA ROSEWOOD MYSTERIES AND OTHER SHORT STORIES
4. THE HOUSE OF EVIL
5. TO TESTIFY FROM THE GRAVE BOOK TWO
6. A POETIC COLLECTION

BLAKE EDWARDS'funeral had begun that morning. HIS half brother BOBBY took care of all the details. BLAKE had been shot to death a few days prior by a US MARSHAL trying to prevent his escape from custody after his court trial. BOBBY had been notified by the local police to come to the morgue to identify BLAKES' body.

BOBBY had been in a veterans' hospital since returning from VIET NAM where he served four years in the GREEN BERETS. HE was hurt and crippled to a degree but was basicaly a guy who could get around.

A few days after the funeral BLAKES'will would be read. BOBBY knew already he no doubt would inherit the business since no other relatives bothered with BLAKE. HE was now so anxious to get this funeral behind him.

Outside the funeral home multiple cars lined the street. BLAKE had had very few friends but, many business associates. HE was admired by some, disliked by others due to his way of doing business.

The funeral director dressed in his black suit and coat and hat directed the visitors to how the traffic pattern was going to be handled. Four motorcyle cops would do the traffic control as they headed for the only cemetary which was across town.

AT eleven a/m the funeral cars with the mourners left the yard. They headed across the main street heading north towards the ancient cemetary. Within a half hour or so they had arrived at the huge cemetary gates.

The main black wrought iron gates were open and in a slow process one by one of the cars filed in. The black clouds overhead made it an eerie day as the funeral proceeded.

The priest arrived at the gravesite. After a brief ceremony each attending party placed a rose on BLAKES' coffin. The crowd funneled out now and dispersed in all directions. BOBBY along with his fiance drove to the north gate. His black MERCEDES reflecting the sunshine now that the clouds had gone.

BOBBY smiled at ADRIANA knowing he was heading out to BLAKES' former beach house. HE knew that after a quick swim, a few drinks, hot sex was the ticket of entertainment on the agenda. HE took after his step brother who always had a pretty woman on his arm. The only difference is that BLAKE had murdered his four former wives and so far BOBBY was doing great with the ladies. BOBBY was not as handsome as BLAKE but his manners and smile and the way he talked made up for it.

Within an hour they drove up to BLAKES' beach house. She loved this place. She loved the ocean, the sunshine, the beautiful scenery and loved the cool waterbed most of all where she could get it on with BOBBY all nite long.

BOBBY parked the car in the driveway and they headed through the patio just as the waves caressed the rocks below adding that romantic touch. The patio door wasn't locked and BOBBY headed straight for the bar. She grabbed her swimsuit from the closet and stripped down getting ready for a swim. HE spotted her nakedness in the door mirror and wanted to take her now as his full erection throbbed against his leg.

HE caught her looking at him through the mirror, her eyes glowing, her heart beating so rapidly as she stood there still stark naked. HE went quickly into the bedroom undressed and in minutes she was down for the count with her long tanned legs parted inviting him to take her now. BOBBY wasted no time going into action giving her a thrill a minute with his caresses. They tumbled on the waterbed until both climaxed with a thundering finish. They paused each lighting a cigarette and sipping on their drinks. She had a powerful set of legsand was drop dead gorgeous. She was only twenty four years old five years younger than BOBBY. They seemed to be very compatible. They had dated for a while now and were a twosome before he joined the army. HE was lucky in love, not as much as BLAKE was but did okay with the ladies.

A few weeks passed and BOBBY attended the reading of his brothers' will. BLAKES' soap business worth millions now was BOBBYS' with him stepping up and becoming its' new ceo. HE now was a millionaire. A yacht was left which was harbored in L/A. Also a private jet was now at his disposal. Dam BOBBY was overwhelmed. Cash and securities amounted in the millions of dollars. BOBBY was set for life. Plus he had to pay BLAKES' funeral expenses from the proceeds of a million dollars policy of a life insurance which named BOBBY as beneficiary. BOBBY was a tycoon now like BLAKE had been. HE could live off the banks' interest as well as the dividends from stocks he had bought, plus he owned controling interest now in the soap company. Not bad for a twenty nine year old he thought as he listened to the lawyer reading the contents of the will

Also the beach house was his now along with his mansion in BEVERLY HILLS BLAKE had bought as a quick money maker investment. And there was more yet including a 1969 CADILAC convertible and a late model black MERCEDES. BOBBY did not have to share any of his inheritance with anyone and REX BLAKES' former lover had committed suicide after learning of BLAKES' death. HIS fortune left by BLAKE went to charity now. BLAKE had surely covered all the bases.

The will finaly read BOBBY left for an important board meeting at the soap company. BOBBY had stock options also to settle up on. BLAKE was no stranger to making investments and had the knack for making profits on anything he touched turn to gold. BLAKE was going to be a hard act to follow.

BOBBY met his limo driver at the main gate and off he went heading to meet with the board the first time. HE figured this would be indeed an experience since he had no time to trace the companies history but this was tossed in his lap immediately because of BLAKE dying. Within an hour BOBBY arrived at the soap company. The board was waiting on the fourth floor in the meeting room. AS BOBBY entered the room he took a deep breath and was surprised by the standing ovation he had received.

"I'M floored by your response" BOBBY replied as he felt the blush color enter his face. The chairman carried out some intro business then introduced BOBBY. "Thank you for the nice reception" BOBBY said as he stood at the podium nervously. "AS you know my brother is deceased and I have been put in charge as C.E,O. to carry this company to the next level". he said as he looked at his audience at the extra large table.

"Due to new product ideas, new packaging, new skills in marketing we can double our bottom line. I believe in five years if projections hit the targets as stated". HE added as the board members applauded his words. BOBBY was glad these members of the board respected his thoughts and his ideals. The meeting lasted three hours. BOBBY was now mentaly exhausted. The last few days had been exhausting with BLAKES' funeral, closing his former place up, and moving into the beach house and he also had to check the mansion in BEVERLY HILLS. HE had his limo driver take him home to the beach house where ADRIANA waited for him. After a half hour drive he was at the foot of the stairs to the white beach house overlooking the ocean with its' scenic view more beautiful than any landscape painting could ever capture.

There she stood at the top of the stairway in her two piece red bikini looking sexy as ever. BOBBY ran up the few steps grabbed her, kissed her and picked her up and carried her to bed again the waterbed would make history of hot sex and torrid love affairs.

ADRIANA removed the top of her swimsuit and tossed it on the floor as BOBBY slid her bottom piece down to her ankles exposing what he wanted and was after. There was no guess work what would take place now as she panted and spread her beautiful tanned legs letting him with a real smooth sensation. They went at it for a couple of hours like two cats caught up in heat. They finaly took a break each lighting a cigarette and BOBBY mixed a couple of drinks. She was surprised by his manners. HEwas as smooth as his step brother with women BLAKE gave him a few pointers. BOBBY adored her nakedness. HE especialy loved looking at her large sized breasts. She was still hot and took sex to a whole new meaning.

After a short rest he flipped her over on her stomach and entered her making her squirm a little but she did not complain but took it as deep as she could. IN minutes she brought herself to a finish like a wild woman. HE finished with her and was content. They rested again both in need of a drink and a cigaretteagain.

IT was time to shower up and dress up for he was taking her to dinner to LUIGIS' the best ITALIAN food in all of the country. Next to sex eating out ranked high on his list. They showered, dressed, and headed out to the car.

BOBBY felt great as he looked her over sitting across from him. She had a white two piece suit with a black blouse and black heels dressed to kill like he always said. IT was an hour drive up the coastline to get to LUIGIS'. She had never been there before but BOBBY had with BLAKE when a double date situation had arisen.

BLAKE had more ladies than most guys, but he was richer, more handsome, more smarter and had resources to spoil the ladies in his circle. Plus he had a yacht, a private jet, nice cars, beautiful homes. HE had it all. The world was his for the taking at any given time.

The night air was extremely warm and the moon shone as big and bright adding a nice touch to their romantic evening. The traffic was light as they continued up the coast. Finaly there it was out on the ledge bigger than life "LUIGIS'". BOBBY pulled into the winding driveway up to the valet parking sign. The attendant smiled and took the keys from BOBBY. BOBBY gave the guy twenty dollars to park his car and hand in hand he and ADRIANA walked up to the door as the doorman opened the door for them.

They smiled at him and went on into be greeted by the hostess. ADRIANA was amazed at the size of the place and how it over looked the ocean. Just about every table was taken even outside on the viranda. The hostess sat them out on the northside patio at a private table alone for them. BOBBY had reserved this spot over the phone so as to impress his date. The more he impressed her the hotter the sex he figured after all he did want to get his cock in her again. She knew very well how to please rich men thats' all she ever had slept with. She liked BOBBY a lot and wanted a deep relationship. She didn't want just dating for sexual pleasure any more. This time it was so different.

BOBBY lit a cigarette as the waiter now approached them taking their drink orders first leaving menus. They decided on what to eat and stared at each other like they were alone on the earth and so deeply in love. HE wanted to take her home and bang her all night. She put her hot hand over his gazing in his eyes lost in lustful thinking as her heart beat quicklyand her womanhood ached wanting him deep inside her later that night if all went well. BOBBY knew by the far away look in her eyes she was ready to spend the night at the mansion in BEVERLY HILLS. She had never been there. BOBBY had a staff of six there most of the time but this week they were off. This would make for a perfect love nest when they were ready.

The waiter brought their food, freshened—the drinks. BOBBY asked her thoughts on the place. She was speechless. HE knew he had indeed impressed this hot bitch. HE could not wait to get in her pants again. She could make a dead man come alive. She was a real hot bitch and that was the bottom line. They had dinner, more drinks, and conversation and the more he looked at her the hornier he got. HE had a long drive back to the mansion yet before he could get to her.

They paid the bill and left. The valet pulled the car up for them. BOBBY tossed him another twenty dollar tip and smiled at the guy and off they went. Traffic was starting to get heavy on the PACIFIC COAST HIGHWAY. BOBBY suggested to stay at a hotel for the night and start out fresh in the morning. She was okay with that being tipsy from to many drinks anyway. BOBBY had a few drinks but seemed to be okay at the moment.

UP ahead was a HILTON. BOBBY pulled into the circular driveway. She was asleep on the passenger seat. BOBBY went inside to the office area. HE got a suite for the night for them on his AMERICAN EXPRESS card. Going back outside he found her awake and told her the room was all set which brought a pretty smile to her tired looking face.

They pulled the car around back and went to their room on the end of the viranda. BOBBY was pleased with the spaciousness of the room. The view was stunning overlooking a tremendous mountain range with a full moon so picturesque. She loved it, the luxury, the gorgeous furniture, the plush red carpeting, the gorgeous custom long window drapes. She felt like a princess in a fairytale. She had never been so excited and pampered ever. She felt BOBBY was perhaps her soul mate. BOBBY called room service for a aged wine and some dinner. A short time later a houseman brought the wine and food. BOBBY was anxious to have dinner and the hotel guy opened the wine and poured two glasses into the flute styled glasses.

They sat and had dinner with lots of conversation. BOBBY eyed her large breasts as she removed her sweater. This was going to be a night to remember for sure. HE poured a second glass of wine for each of them, smiling warmly as he did so. She was starting to relax a little. HE wanted her to unwind to put her in the mood for hot sex. HE sipped his wine slowly tasting the fineness of it. She lit a cigarette and turned on the tv. She was now getting drowsy for it had been a long day.

HE wanted sex wheter she was tired or not. She laid there, her eyes heavy in need of sleep. BOBBY figured let her nap for a few hours then pound the hell out of her with as much sex as she could endure. HE was horny as he checked out her breasts so lucious yet not so available due to she was beat. Later on he'd make up for it he was sure. She now drifted off to sleep. HE covered her with a blanket and turned on the a/c. HE turned on the tv to the news channel. TO his surprise there was a old news clip about his brothers'death just about a year ago and how a US MARSHAL shot and killed him during a try to escape from custody. BOBBY felt bad seeing the story rehashed again. HE promised himself he'd have that US MARSHAL killed by some hired killer friend of his family.

Several weeks later after making a phone call and money arrangement the marshall was found shot to death in his home. BOBBY had revenged his brothers' death after all what was brotherly love for anyway ?HE smiled to himself about it as he watched the news.

Adriana awoke looking around the room for BOBBY. HE was in the shower getting ready for a night of bliss. She got the hint and got undressed lying nude across the queen sized bed her long tanned legs spread eagled showing her inner pink womans' pussy. She was ready, had ideas of what was coming next. HE had been patient waiting half the night and needed a release soon.

Several minutes later he came into the room, his after shave adding its' fragrance to the air. She reached out for him as he bent to get his cigarettes on the nightstand. HE lit one and walked to the bar and made them each a dry martini.

HE was a gentleman no doubt, suave, smooth, handsome and ready to pounce on her. HE gazed at her nudity with lust filled EYES, a glowing warmth, a need to have sex, driven like an animal in heat. HE sat down on the edge of the bed sipping his drink and smoking his imported cigarette. HE had the world by the ass and he knew it.

HE bent to kiss her and caressed her waiting hardened nipples so pink, so perfect, so real perky waiting for his tongue to pleasure them which she loved. SHE opened her long legs wider her inner thighs red hot ready, willing and able to take him deep into her caverns of love. That was it, that magic, his touch, his commands verbaly talking dirty turned her on. She rolled over onto her stomach, spreading her legs and propping her ass upward so he could enter her easily from the rear. HE shoved his hard penis into her making her yell for more, turning her on like a raging animal in heat. She was loving every minute never before had she had sex with a man as good as this guy. She was sure she found her soul mate. They seemed perfect for each other

FOR being in a relationship for a short span of time they were doing well. She was very responsive to his wants and needs. IT was like she could read his mind knowing exactly sex wise what he expected of her. HER moves turned him on. HEwas gentle as they moved into a different position. SHE was open to suggestion when it came to new sex acts-that would blow her mind.

Finaly. they had to rest. They each lit a cigarette and he poured two more martinis making this moment so special. She gazed into his eyes with a lustful look, her lips wet with desire, her heart beating out of control. She was ready, willing and able to go another round right now. She repositioned herself as he slid above her placing himself perfectly. HER body was hot to the touch. HER eyes glowed bright with the look of love. IT was a steamy session then they were forced to rest from exhaustion. They slept in each others' arms.

ADRIANA woke up first. She was cuddled up to BOBBYS' muscular arms. She looked down at him. She spotted his penis and started to rub it to get it erect. Sperm rolled off the tip making her fingers sticky. HE awoke and realized his erection was ready to fire away at her. They slipped into a nice position and he took her to the outer limits of her orgasm. HE knew how to satisfy the ladies. HE was a lot like BLAKE his half brother. She loved it as much as he did. She never had sex like she had with BOBBY. She kept thinking that he was really her soul mate. ADRIANA liked BOBBY a lot and he too was crazy about her. HE had turned her on like she had never been turned on before. They made love until they were so tired they had to quit.

BOBBY showered and dressed in white slacks and a flowered shirt. She smiled at him as she went to shower. After a long hot shower she dressed in a nice dungaree outfit. BOBBY figured they'd go for a drive up the coast. The weather was balmy but no rain was forcasted so they took the sports car. With the top down they drove onto the main road.

BOBBY was glad to get away for a while lately the business had taken up a lot of his time. ADRIANA loved spending endless hours with him relaxing, dining out as well as sightseeing, the beaches GOD with him life was so fast paced but she loved every minute of it. They were like two teens in love for the first time ever. LIFE was good. BOBBY familiar with the area took the nice scenic route. The warm breezes added natures' touch to a beautiful blue sky. IT was a real perfect night for a drive up the coast again.

She remained quiet for the most part as she listened to the FM channel on his radio. She was very relaxed now that she had her fullfillment of her sexual desires. She was still horney enough to get laid again and soon she thought.

BOBBY smiled at her as he now reached for his cigarettes. HE lit one as he now changed lanes heading in another direction. NOW he headed north heading to the mountain area. BLAKE his deceased brother had bought a cabin deep tnto the mountains. BOBBY had been there once before years ago when BLAKE first bought it. IT was a two bedroom cabin deep in the woods on private property belonging to BLAKE. IT was a great get away spot when seclusion was needed. BOBBY had figured she'd love it. HE owned it free and clear due to his brothers'will.

HE owned also the mansion in BEVERLY HILLS and the beach house in MALIBU. BOBBY could impress his lover that's for sure. Finaly after a few hours of driving BOBBY pulled off the main road onto a private road that lead to into the woods. IN a short time they drove up to the cabin. IT was an older built one but well kept up. The palm trees hovered over it like a protective mother. They entered through the front door. BOBBY picked her up and carried her over the threshold trying to be comical. She giggled as he pushed the large door aside. The main room had white carpeting, a beautiful slate gray fireplace, ruby colored drapes, a beautiful slender tvand stereo set along with a small bar type refrigarator. IT spelt out comfort for sure

She explored the bedrooms as well as the oversized bathroom. She was stunned by the beauty of the deck that wrapped itself around the log cabin. She knew BOBBY was wealthy after seeing this place. HE owned several acres of land surrounding the dwelling as well. HE use to hunt deer with his brother here he told her. Those were in their younger days. The guys were always doing something.

BOBBY walked over to the small bar at the end of the main room and set up drinks for them. HE figured she'd get drunk, have wild hot sex and pass out. They toasted to their happiness. BOBBY refilled her glass smiling at her as he gazed at her large grapefruit sized breasts. HE wanted those and wanted them right then and there. HE handed her a drink and made his move to grab her breasts. She did not resist as he opened her blouse and took them from the red laced bra. HER big nipples were erect and rose colored, so beautiful he thought to himself.

IN no time they stripped and were going at it like two mated animals in heat. She wanted oral sex on her for a while which made her hotter than any fire in HELL. HE obliged her quickly. HER big black hairy pussy wet, but ready for action beyond his imagination. HE satisfied her to some degree and made love to her for a while longer. Finaly they fell asleep in each others' arms.

Hours later BOBBY awoke. ADRIANA slept quietly. HE gazed at her realizing how much he really cared about her. She was amazingly his soul mate he thought about their relationship. Who knew months later he would have strong feelings for hcr. HE told himself when they first met that this was a fling only no tie in to a real relationship but the situation grew more intense, more real, more loving, more sex too. They loved each other more than he expected. Now there was no turning back, no running from it for the reality was he was falling deeply in love with her.

BOBBY felt something magic between them that he had never experienced ever before. AT last he had found true love, a reason for existing, a reason to seek new tomorrows, a reason to create loving memories. HEwas going to build his future with ADRIANA. IF she continued to make him happy so be it he said to himself.

AT last he was happy with his life. She fit in perfectly. LIFE was great. HIS brother left a fortune he'd never live long enough to spend. IF he should marry her he'd be able to give her anything her heart desired. She deserved it after all she was his sexual godess and satisfied his every need always searching for new ways to drive his sexual needs clear over the edge always keeping it fresh and exciting.

She knew his ex-girlfriend who told her his likes and dislikes. The two ladies were students at the local community college. Now ADRIANA was in the drivers' seat as the saying goes so she had to meet the criteria to satisfy BOBBY. BOBBY was easy to satisfy. A woman who gave herself freely with sexual favors pretty much kept the millionaire content.

The next day they headed back with plans to get to the mansion and remain there for a few days because BOBBY had business in the area to take care of. BOBBY constantly found ways to add to his cash flow. HE was a sharp business guy, learned well from his brother BLAKE. They both had the midas touch when it came to wealth. Everything they touched seemed to turn to gold.

After a two and a half hour drive they pulled into the circular driveway. There it stood the largest mansion on the top of the mountain. She could not believe the view from where she stood. She could see all of BEVERLY HILLS. The sunshine was radiant dancing on the beautiful all grey stone home. She stood there taking in the gorgeous view as well as the freshest air at that elevation. HE now took a bunch of keys from his jeans pocket shutting off the alarm system first and then unlocked the door to the most amazing home she'd ever saw. This made the beach house look like a shack in comparison. The foyer was awesome with a diamond cut chandelier hanging over the entrance way. The plush red carpeting was breath taking, and the drapes so beautiful with white and gold trimmings enhancing the rooms' splendor. The all white leather futuristic styled furniture added that special appeal of elegance.

The greystone fireplace really set up the romantic touch to the elaborate settings. She could not wait to see the rest of the place. BOBBY took her by the hand and waltzed her through the house.

The kitchen was inviting with a center isle stove, multiple cabinets, chrome refrigerator, multiple windows which allowed the moonlight in abundance. She just could not believe her eyes. She came from a poor immigrant family living in furnished rooms most of her life. This was an amazing experience for her. She had never known luxury at its'peak of greatness like this ever before. The bathrooms were immense in size both having a jacuzzi of their own. The outside patio wrap around was amazing with its'view of just about all of BEVERLY HILLS.

BOBBY took her by the hand walking her to the master bedroom after all needed just a quickie to wet his appetite. She was willing as he caressed her big breasts from behind her and pushed her gently towards the large waterbed. IN minutes she laid there half nude with her slacks down to her ankles. She kicked them off to the floor. She spread her legs showing him the beautiful hairy patch awaiting his large member to enter her. She was hot, ready to go, to build on her greatest fantasies. HE gently entered her. She leaned back and took him inside her as deep as he could reach. IN no time she reached multiple climaxes making her yell out loud to go deeper and faster reaching her peek in orgasms. HE gave her as much as he could being gentle as he could. After an hour or so both laid there exhausted.

HE lit a cigarette and handed it to her and lit one for himself. She could not believe what a loving guy he was. She loved the attention.

HE knew how to pamper her. She knew how to deliver what he wanted in return to be real spoiled. They were well mated for each other. They seemed to know what each other was thinking.

There was a magic between them. BOBBY never met anyone like her before. This babe was so perfect that he could not believe it. They were wildly in love already in the short time they had known each other. With the perfection of this relationship BOBBY had thought about it. HEwould propose marriage before someone tries to pull them apart. HE wanted her as his wife someday but right now they were building their relationship seeing where it leads to.

Morning arrived. BOBBY had left early attending a board meeting. ADRIANA was asleep yet. BOBBY left her a note that he'd return sometime after one p/m. BOBBY had to be there this morning to talk about buying out a smaller soap company for about a million dollars. HE wasn't sure wheter the board would go along with him on this deal or not but he held 80%of the stock so his ideas were rarely challenged or turned down for he had the power to do as he saw fit just like his brother BLAKE had done prior.

The board had gathered already as BOBBY entered the room. Everyone stood up as he took his seat at the head of the table. HE was well liked by most members where BLAKE had made enemies along the way stepping on people who helped him be a success. BLAKE could care less who liked him or did not like him for he was agressive and that was the bottom line.

BOBBY on the other hand was kinder, understanding, sought approval from others and wanted the support of others. HEdid not have the expertise BLAKE had to run a multimillion dollar company

HE was eager to learn and be better than BLAKE was. The meeting lasted just about three hours with everyone on the same page to buy out the smaller company but lower the purchase price some. BOBBY grabbed his attache case and headed out the door to the elevator.

BOBBY was anxious to get home to ADRIANA for a few hours in the sack would sure make his new day special. IT was an hour drive back to the mansion. Depending on traffic it could be a longer ride home,. HE entered the thruway onto the main highway ramp joining many other cars. The sun was going down, with a nice warn breeze as he let the red top of the convertible. HE lit a cigarette and turned on the news trying to relax as traffic picked up. IT was around noon now one of the most busiest times of the day. Traffic snarled to a halt.

HE now dialed ADRIANA on his cell phone. After two rings she answered. She was surprised by the call. She was preparing a nice lunch of steaks, fries and salad for the afternoon. They spoke briefly and he hung up. Traffic moved again. After an hour and a half of heavy traffic he pulled into his circular driveway. HE was glad to be home. She met him at the door in a two piece yellow bikini small enough to push her boobs upward so he could see the red hardened nipples. HE was instantly turned on as he gave her a nice kiss. She set the patio table up. The steaks were hot off the grill, the salad fresh cut just as he liked it and a bottle of wine had been chilled along with two wine glasses. HE was surprised by this nice set up for lunch but in his thoughts he wanted hot sex with her.

HE watched her big breasts heave up and down. She was horny no doubt. She had missed her morning quickie. HEwas hungry but would rather toss her onto the waterbed, spread her legs as far out and give her what she craved for a hot cock and loads of hot sperm.

They ate quietly with a little bit of conversation. HE told her about buying out the smaller soap company if they could only agree on a price. She smiled and told him it would all work out in the end. HE knew she was right. They finished lunch. HE poured two glasses of chilled wine and granted a toast to their relationship. She was starting to feel the effects of the wine.

She asked him to remove her bikini top and as he did her big tits bounced like two grapefruits. HE grabbed the nipple of her right breast and kissed it gently. The nipple hardened on his lips. HE pulled off her bikini bottom and in moments was rocking her world on the cool waterbed. She shrieked with lustful dirty words as she took him inside her like she had never known ever before.

BOBBY always wondered wheter she had put out for a lot of guys before he came along. BOBBY had it all. HEwas a good lover, had money, had homes, had airplanes, had top selling cars, had the world by the ass for sure. She knew she hit pay dirt when her and BOBBY had hooked up. She was going to ride this gravy train as far as she could. UNLESS BOBBY grew tired of her she was his sex godess forever. HER plan was to get him to marry her so she could have even more than she was getting already. With time things would change for BOBBY liked to keep things fresh. BOBBY wasn't sure wheter he was in love with her or not. She really cared about him.

They made love like two young teens. She could do things with her body that would turn him on instantly. She had a body of a swimsuit model. HE adored her breasts, always wanting to squeeze them and kiss them with his hot hands and lips. She loved all the attention he gave her. TO BOBBY she was a good piece of ass and she knew how to please him in every way. She loved pleasing her man and reaping the rich benefits from the relationship. She was a cougar as the saying goes and he was a wolf so together they were a hell of a couple. After a real physical workout they relaxed with a glass of wine and of course a cigarette.

She laid there relaxed, her body sweaty, her hair messybut feeling loved by the one, the only BOBBY EDWARDS. She finished her cigarette and her wine and headed for the shower. BOBBY poured himself more wine. HE had planned to join her in the shower in just a few minutes. HE started to feel the effects of the wine as he headed for the bathroom. HE opened the bathroom door and opened the shower door.

She smiled as she handed him the soap and a wash cloth. HE knew right away what she wanted. HE washed her big boobs watching the big brown nipples get hard as his hands scrubbed them gently. She liked being pampered. She grabbed his cock and gently ran her hand down to his hairy balls giving him a instant erection. HE dripped cum from his tip onto her arm as she guided her hand up and down on his cock.

HE was ready to take her on. She leaned in close to him her body hot with desire not wanting to wait any longer to place his hot cock inside her wet pussy. HE picked her up tossed her against the tile wall as the hot water blasted covering both of them. The shower steamed up quickly, their bodies interwining so tightly. SHE eased in closer BOBBY going deeper inside her his hot cock throbbing easy ready to shoot his sperm up her hot hole.

She was ready no doubt as she closed her eyes savoring the moment in her mind. IN minutes it was over. The shower ran continuosly on them down some as BOBBY turned the cooler water up some. They toweled each other laughing about their little episode in the tight sized shower. They headed for the living room wrapped in their white terry robes.

BOBBY mixed two drinks. BOBBY handed her a drink. She lit a cigarette. They were quite relaxed now. BOBBY clicked on the tv. to check the local news. The surprise news was that his company was in the middle of a hot debate in regards taking over another small soap company. BOBBY laughed as the story unfolded briefly. ADRIANA did not comment on the story afraid she'd be out of line to say anything. The next news story was a murder that took place in LAGUNA HILLS. A womans'body washed up on the shore. She had been a community college student who lived in LAGUNA HILLS for a few years now. The coroner claimed she was pregnant. ADRIANA didn't know but BOBBY knew the victim She had worked part time at his company but he did not want to disclose this fact to her. HE hardly knew the young girl. HE had interviewed her, hired-her and that pretty much was the bottom line. HE switched channels looking into a sports report. HEwas a sports fanatic. HE loved baseball most of all. ADRIANA liked hockey. They had something in common. They sat there watching the local news. BOBBY poured two more drinks as he started to talk some.

HE seemed concerned about his company buying out the other soap company. This was his very first dealing in a buyout. She smiled as she listened to her lover discuss the business world. HE fascinated her by the way he talked.

She liked being with a real smart guy. She was pretty sharp herself and could really hold conversations with the best of them. HE was amazed by her and her very wordly ways. Their relationship was getting more and more interesting. She wanted their relationship to work no matter how hard she had to work at it.

She liked living the the high life. She was spoiled wrotten. HE bought her jewelry, a car, perfumes imported from all over the world. Plus she lived at the mansion as well as the beach house. The lady had it made. She had the world by the ass. AS long as she kept him happy she'd lead the life other women would die for. BOBBY had a string of ladies in his life but when ADRIANA showed up that was it for the others. HE became a one woman man.

She was everything he wanted in one lady and conquered his heart. She was in line perhaps to be his first wife if all went well. SO far so good. She would love to be MRS. BOBBY EDWARDS. She'd have the world at her doorstep. She'd be the envy of every woman. She'd be in the limelight. She'd live the life she had always dreamed of. She'd get anything she ever wanted. She'd go from being an average gal to a wealthy woman. Nice life if you can get it as the saying goes. She'd finaly make it to the top being MRS. BOBBY EDWARDS.

She'd be the envy of of everyone around her and in the highlight in her new society circles position. HEY she worked her way into his world and now will reap the rewards of their relationship. This chick was smart. She knew how to manipulate men using her body as their reward and in turn got showered with gifts galore. She was going to play this game to the finish. She did love BOBBY so that had counted for something.

That afternoon BOBBY suggested to hang out at the beach house and swim in the OLYMPIC sized pool. BOBBY loved being at the poolwhile using his computer to conduct business. HE received several hundred e-mail a day due to how big his business had grown. When BLAKE was alive he too handled a lot of business from his home. These two guys had the world by the ass. They had earned millions with their motivating factors of running the soap company. NO family could compare to theirs. For generations old money made new money. They had no competition any where. They were the number one producer of soap products in the U.S.A. at the time.

BOBBY ran his business pretty much daily from his patio deck, by the pool either at the MALIBU house or from his mansion in BEVERLY HILLS. Once a week he'd show up at his office unannounced in CENTURY CITY and shake the nerves of his employees. HE had hired several managers to take care of things at the office and the soap factory was run by his cousin OLIVIA EDWARDS, a tyrant who was as tough as a box of nails. She was a former D/I in the U. S. MARINES. She was no pushover and had served hard times in VIET NAM formerly and had escaped from a P. O. W, camp. She was a survivor. She took her military skills to become a top notch general manager for BOBBY. HE was pleased with her. They talked daily on the phone and e-mailed the issues important enough to be handled. Now as he and ADRIANA hung out at the pool life was great.

After several hours at poolside BOBBY set up the gas grill. ADRIANA loved cooking out and was ready to release her first cooking book in L/A. BOBBY brought out two enourmous steaks from the freezer. She went inside and made a giant bowl of salad. That done she joined him for a drink at poolside. The sun was just setting as they toasted themselves to a long life of happiness.

The warm breezes caressed the air as the ocean nearby kissed the rocks below the ledge of the beach house sending salt fragrance into the air. ITwas a romantic setting for an intimate dinner on the patio. SEAGULS filled the air hovering around searching for food as they looked skyward. The night sky darkened and the beach house lights littered the shoreline.

After a few more rounds of booze she was getting playful and wanted to play adult games on the cool waterbed. IN moments he carried her to his master bedroom anticipating a sex workout. HE placed her softly on the cool waterbed. She sat up, slipped out of her blouse, undid her bra letting her grapefruit sized breasts dangle in his face getting his attention quickly. IN minutes they were in a compromising position with her yelling louder and louder the deeper he penetrated her. She had boundless energy when it came to sexual activity. HE caressed her large breasts, her nipples hard as a rock wanting his mouth waiting hotly to be sucked by this wild man. She adjusted her position as she wildly french kissed him. IT was hours later that they finaly rested. She was sweaty, but satisfied, he the same. Their love life was high powered always fresh, always new and exciting. She knew how to hold his attention.

They showered. Then slipped into their matching white terry cloth robes. HE made a couple of drinks for them. She lit herself a cigarette as she gazed at him lounging there half asleep from all the physical action. HE lit an imported cigar leaning back in his lounge chair relaxing.

BOBBY was a more laid back C.e.o. His big brother BLAKE was always at the office on top of things. BOBBY didn't make the business control him. HE did what he had to do but put no extra effort in for he felt he was wealthy enough and didn't care about the next day. Life would take care of him for after all he was BOBBY EDWArds millionaire.

BOBBY mixed two more drinks just as the phone rang. HE picked the call up after a few rings. The voice on the line was that of a former girlfriend of his. BOBBY walked into the house his cell phone tightly to his ear.

Sherry TAYLOR his ex-lover now pregnant with his child demanded a large sum of money for future expenses. BOBBY promised her a call back the next morning with more details how she could collect. HE lied to her. HE made a quick call to a hit man he used to rub out unwanted people. IT would cost him some serious bucks but he felt it was worth it to dispose of the potential problems she'd bring to his door. IF he did not have her bumped off she'd expose him to the media and drag him through the mud of society demands.

HE made the call, gave the hit man her name and address, scanned her photo via a e-mail and wired $10,000 to the guys' account. IT was set up to bump her off the following morning. HE felt good, powerful, glad that she'd be taken care of.

Meanwhile ADRIANA was asleep on the lounge chair on the deck. The moon was full now, the warm breezes filled the air. There was a hint of rain coming in the air. HE did not disturb her but reached for his box of cigars and lit one as he laid back in his lounge chair. HE felt content with himself. HE needed sex but would take care of his needs later on that night.

The next morning all over the news was the story of the murdered woman SHERRY TAYLOR. Her body was found at the bottom of a cliff in what was left of a burning car. She had been seven months pregnant. There was no mention of her relationship with BOBBY at all which obviously made him happy. Problem resolved. After all when your rich you can buy solutions to any problem.

HE switched tv channels. The media was having a field day with the young womans' story. The gory photos showed the car wreckage at the end of the canyon. Again no mention of his name. IN the meantime ADRIANA awoke and came into the tv room. She questioned the death of the woman and BOBBY assured her it was none of their business. HE told her chances are bad brakes failed and over the edge she went. She just gave him an odd stare expecting to hear more of a compassionate remark.

HE lit a cigar and nervously mixed two drinks. ADRIANA kept real quiet not wanting to get argumentive at all over the incident. After all let the media hype play it up this is what sells the news. The media loved stories of death and mysterious deaths. IT would be months of an investigation but BOBBY wasn't worried at all for he had an alibi with his new gal at the beach house. The EDWARDS boys always covered their tracks with solid alibis. They were not only rich, they were clever and also bought an alibi or two where needed. Most of the towns' judges would never go up against the EDWARDS' family for they supported the judges job when it was time to vote and cash passed among the right hands in order to put that judge in office even though everyone had a hunch these millionaires supported the votes to go the way they wanted them to go. The EDWARDS were very rich and powerful like the KENNEDYS.

NO one would ever dispute the votes or ask for a recount. IT would not be healthy to do so. Politics in this state were dirty. These wealthy folks lived so different than the rest of the population

BOBBYS' phone rang. The main office phoned to give him his stock report. HE asked them to fax it over to him. The soap company stocks had gone from $43. 00 a share to $69.

00 overnight on news of the upcoming merger that was nearly completed. HIS company would be in 98%controling interest from here on. IT was a nice increase for BOBBY owned a few thousand shares. HE was not only the C.e.o. but a wealthy man to boot. HE knew his business, knew how to get rid of the competition.

The next day being SATURDAY BOBBY decided they should take a drive up the coast. HE was going to surprise ADRIANA by looking at the homes for sale on THE PACIFIC COAST HIGHWAY—a good ride from his home in MALIBU. HE figured that if they got married he'd get her a nice home along the beach front perhaps the area known as REDONDO BEACH which had condos for sale right on the ocean.

HE told her to get dressed that they were going to get some breakfast somewhere. She was pleased by that bit of news. She dressed casualy in jeans, a nice tight western shirt—with boots. HE smiled at her as he closed the doors behind them. They took the black MERCEDES. BObby liked that car the best of what he owned. HE pulled onto the main road and headed in the direction of the coast. She put her window down allowing the warm breezes to caress her tanned face. BOBBY looked over at her smiled and reached for his cigars

Traffic was light as they reached the entrance to the freeway IT was almost noon as they headed east towards the beach. The scenic route from the high elevation was breath taking. The sky overhead filled with seaguls swooping up and down diving for fish along the coastline. She lit a cigarette, smiled at him leaning back in the seat relaxing. BOBBY looked at her for a moment—her boobs so large like a pair of cantolopes. HE wanted to make love to her but there was no spot to pull off for a quickie. Her ruby lips looked inviting and he wanted to french kiss her so badly. HE smiled that devilish way that captured her heart.

They drove into the canyon, then north towards a the shore. She was napping as he drove up the scenic coastline. Finaly an hour passed and he pulled up in front of a realtors' office. ADRIANA awoke from her nap, stretched a bit, smiled and lit a cigarette.

ROBERT LANSING the owner of the real estate firm greeted them quickly. BOBBY shook hands with the guy, introduced ADRIANA quickly and in a short time they were headed out to see a place that ROBERT had recommended to BOBBY via of the internet. The drive was short and they pulled up in front of this gorgeous beach house tucked away in a canyon overlooking THE PACIFIC OCEAN.

BOBBY and ADRIANA followed MR. LANSING as he guided them up the floral trimmed pathway to this monumentive style home. IN the rear of it was an OLYMPIC pool. The home overlooked the ocean from a high ledge warding privacy when needed. The kitchen was spacious with cabinets galore, brand new appliances and a view that only MOTHER NATURE could provide. The living room was shy a few feet of a ballroom at a night club again windows with a view that was breath taking. The bathroom was immense with real gold fixtures with a full shower as well as a jacuzzi. Moving forward the master bedroom was gigantic with its'own fireplace. BOBBY was amazed at its'size and ADRIANA was totaly swept away by its'beauty.

This was a house built for a princess for sure. ROBERT asked questions and BOBBY said he liked the place but wanted to see one more before making a buying decision ROBERT agreed to show them another beach house along the MALIBU shores. They were on their way to view another place of luxury living.

IN a short time they arrived with ROBERT—at a mansion up on the highest elevation they ever saw before. ROBERT parked the car and hurried around to open doors for his clients. ROBERT had been to this property several other times. BOBBY held ADRIANAS'hand as they followed ROBERT up the winding staircase. ITwas an incredible view from the top step. You could see all of MALIBU and other parts of southern CALIFORNIA. ADRIANA was captured by the beauty surrounding this piece of property.

ROBERT unlocked the lock box, got the key and unlocked the door. The sun was setting now as they took in the view from the large living room window. The living room was so lavious with its' fireplace, full length red velour drapes and white carpet highlighted by red and white furniture ROBERT moved them forward to the master bathroom with its'own jacuzzi. Next the master bedroom in blue decor with high cathederal ceilings. HE moved them now out to the patio deck—the view breath taking. The panorama view just was totaly amazing. This was mother nature at her best. The three of them made small talk, then BOBBY asked the price. ROBERT told him it was a steal at 4. 1 million dollars. BOBBY asked about a straight cash offer in regards to this wonderful home...

ROBERT told BOBBY he had to check with the owners if he was really serious about taking this. BOBBY did not flinch but demanded ROBERT contact the owner right there and then for BOBBY played no games, nor pulled any punches. HEwas the real deal. BOBBY had the cash so he was in the position to call the shots. Money was no object. HE wanted to show ADRIANA that he could buy her the world. She had no idea how rich he was. ROBERT wanted a decision wheter BOBBY was definetly going to buy the place if he could get a better cash price. The guy called the owner and a price was negotiated that made all parties happy.

BOBBY asked ADRIANA if she'd be happy living in this beautiful home of course she said yes with a broad smile. Now all there was left was to arrange a payment, a closing, legal respond all would work out. ROBERT the realtor would work things out. BOBBY had the cash, the guy selling the place had the right price and the realtor would make a killer commission.

IT would be a win-win situation. ADRIANA was overwhelmed by how BOBBY talked about the price of the mansion like it was pocket change. She had no idea how rich he really was. HE never ever gave her a hint about his wealth.

HIS finances were kept on a personal level. She never inquired either feeling it was none of her affairs to ask or talk about it. BOBBY would share info if he wanted to.

The three of them looked over the house one more time but BOBBY was truly convinced that this place was perfect for he and ADRIANA if they married, which soon he was going to pop the question. The three made small talk as they returned to the realtors'car.

BOBBY was excited, so proud he'd made a decision on this beautiful estate and again money wasn't an issue. Just like his deceaesd brother BLAKE money never was an issue. They had old money they hadn't spent yet. Like the KENNEDYS money was in abundance. The realtor drove them back to his office where BOBBY signed a few documents. Then BOBBY and his lover left heading to the beach house.

BOBBY was horny wanting to get ADRIANA on his big waterbed. She was a little anxious to for some sexual activity as well. The weather was pure gorgeous, warm breezes caressing their faces as they drove along the coastlinewith the convertible top down.

She reached for his right hand to make the connection. His mind was focused on the purchase of the new place. She remained quiet the rest of the trip. IF he was concerned with the buying of the new place she'd have to be understanding. She did not want to anger him. Perhaps he was under stress with his soap business booming and the demands put on him by the board of directors. Even though he was the C.e.o. he had to answer to them. HE did not like it but had to live with it like his brother.

Finaly they reached the beach house. HE was in a hurry to get her in bed. She was anxious too. She loved having sex. She was turned on easily and could go at it for hours of foreplay and good old hot sexual activity. She loved sex with BOBBY and he satisfied her better than her former husband of many years. IT gave her the feeling of control over her male lover with her ways in bed.

AS they drove into the driveway they noticed a black car parked in front of the house. Two men approached them who readily identified themselves as F.B.I. agents from L/A. They were following up on BLAKE EDWARDS 'dealings with insurance companies. BOBBY explained that he had no idea what BLAKE had done when he had bought life insurance policies on his former wives then suddenly they were murdered and he had collected millions after their deaths. The F.B.I. told BOBBY that if BLAKE were alive he would have gone to jail for over twenty years. BOBBY was glad when they left. Now he and ADRIANA went inside.

ADRIANA wondered what kind of man BLAKE had been and what kind of family she was getting involved with. She was hoping BOBBY wasn't a bad guy and just put on an act of being kind and considerate. She felt nervous now that she heard the conversation between BOBBY and the F.B.I. BOBBY suddenly was quiet, lost in thought. HE now owed her an explanation but, it wasn't going to be easy.

BOBBY went inside to the bar mixed two drinks and sat down nervously next to her. HE handed her a drink, sweat on his forehead now wondering how to explain his brother BLAKE. BOBBY did not know all the facts on BLAKE— because BOBBY had been in the army and away in VIET NAM. BLAKE ran the business alone, so who knew how dirty he was. BLAKE was dead now and that part of the EDWARDS' family history was better off forgotten about.

BOBBY hesitated to say anything now but the look of concern showed in ADRIANAS'eyes. HE did not know where to begin to air his brothers'dirty laundry. She sat there in total silence, her STOMACH nervous over the situation. HE took her hand, looked into big hazel colored eyes, wanting to open up, but sat tight lipped. HE really did not know enough about BLAKE to really comment. HE had been in the military for years, stayed in touch once in a while. They were never really close. She sat there patiently not knowing what to say or expect to hear if anything. HE poured two more drinks trying to build his courage, trying to give some form of telling her something, anything but how was the question. HE mixed two drinks handed her one forcing a smile realisticaly he was full of tension since talking with the F.B.I.

HE really could not help them that much-brother BLAKE had got involved with illegal activity and paid his debt to society by being gunned down in the street by the U. S. MARSHAL, who had transported him to court. NOW BOBBY who is honest and is very active in the company he runs lives in his brothers' shadow. IT makes him feel guilty but he does the best he can to convince people he was nothing like his brother BLAKE.

HE smiled at her nervously, sweat building on his brow, he felt ill at ease not knowing how to explain his brother to ADRIANA. Finaly he took a deep breath, reached for her hand, looked deeply into large hazel eyes, stuttering some to get the words out. HE had no idea where to start this conversation. She smiled warmly as he held her hand so tenderly trying to say something, anything.

After he took another deep breath he said he was sorry for what she had heard and how he wasn't that close in a relationship with his brother trying to make her understand his side of the lenghty story. She said nothing just squeezed his hand in hers which showed her support and belief in what he said. BOBBY continued his story, now lighting a cigarette to ward off his nervousness. She was easy to talk to which made him relax. Now she listened intently as he spoke the evil truth about BLAKE his deceased brother.

BOBBY just knew bits and pieces of his brothers' life and rumors that found their way around. HE never had a intimate relationship with BLAKE. HE had spent years away in VIET NAM in the special forces so he lost track of what was happening on the home front. Life away in the jungles of VIET NAM was so distant—all that mattered there was survival. Now here he sat with ADRIANA with her questions not really knowing how to respond. She sat motionless as he contiplated how to open up the conversation. HE had to hide certain things from her for BLAKES' reputation hung out there like dirty laundry for all to see. HE broke it to her as gently as he could. She seemed to be understanding not holding him responsible for the life his brother had lived.

BOBBY was glad he opened up to her. She'd sooner or later would find out the truth. ITwas a great relief now that it was out in the open. HE made two more drinks and suggested they'd make love. She agreed. She was hot between her legs. She stripped off her blouse and tossed it onto the big leather chair. Her black laced bra was tossed over her shoulder landing on a large pillow. She dropped her jeans to the floor. She was hot and ready. She was right there for the taking. She never wore panties so it was show time.

BOBBY was so pleased with her as he laid her back on the waterbed, she spreading her legs as he lowered her into the right position. IT was only minutes before he entered her. She was wet with desire. She didn't even flinch. She just laid there enjoying every moment of bliss he could provide. HE pushed himself inside her until she asked him to stop because it hurt. Finaly it was over. She was sore but not satisfied. HE was happy for sure. They kissed tenderly for a moment.

AS night approached they showered together, then relaxed with a drink and of course a cigarette. BOBBY turned on the tv. HE loved the news channel and sports. She sat there quietly sipping her drink why he amused himself on the sports updates. HE finished his drink and went to the bar and mixed two more for them. Drinking seemed to relax him. After a few drinks both of them felt at ease.

She suggested she'd cook some steaks on the outside grilland since this was southern CALIFORNIA weather wasn't a problem. HE went to the deep freezer grabbed a couple of filet mignons. HE told her in the kitchen there were large potatoes and onions. She headed to the kitchen fussing about. IN the meantime he set up the gas grill. The sun was getting to set now, with warm winds-the evening was starting off smoothly.

BOBBY fixed the grill and headed to the barwhen his cell phone rang. The caller was from headquarters of his soap company. The nervous voice spoke quickly about the F.B.I. had been there investigating his brother BLAKE again. They were trying hard to uncover whatever dirt they could. The F.B.I. were not going to back off until they solve the case of BLAKE EDWARDS'and insurance fraud. Even though BLAKE was dead the F.B.I. would find some way to recoupe the millions that BLAKE made illegaly. BOBBY did not like this whole situation. BLAKE may have been crooked but BOBBY was honest. This was really bad publicity for his company. BOBBY hung up the phone terrified with the news that the F.B.I. had been to his headquarters.

Now he had to keep the hype out of the medias' hands for bad publicity could destroy him as well as his company. HE lit a cigarette and sat motionless, his mind wandering with what action to take next to protect his company.

From the patio ADRIANA called him. HE went out to the patio deck almost in a confused state of mind. She smiled warmly as she now turned the steaks over. HE forced a smile not wanting to let on that he was worried sick over this mess BLAKE had brought about with his dishonesty.

BOBBY went inside to the bar to mix two drinks. HE lit a cigarette just as the phone rang HE let the call go to voicemail for the time being. HE just did not want to deal with anything else. HE went back onto the patio. ADRIANA was setting up the corn rack on the grill. BOBBY loved corn on the grill. She placed several baked potatoes along side the steaks. She was quite the cookto BOBBYS' surprise for he looked at her as his lover more than anything. HE handed her a drink and they toasted to their relationship. ADRIANA had removed her blouse and her red bikini top sure got his attention. After all she did have a nice set of boobs that looked perky in that skimpy top.

She was a sex kitten alright. She had beautiful legs, solid breast like a teenage gal, gorgeous lips fueled like no other woman he had ever had prior. She was hot and he wanted to take her right there on the patio. She kept on cooking ignoring his stares, knowing very well what he had on his mind.

SEX was going to wait a while at least until she got supper ready for them. BOBBY just wanted a quickiebut knew that this was not the right time. HE lit a cigarette trying to relax a bit. HE checked out her rear end as she bent to turn off the lp tank.

GOD he wanted her so badly at this moment. HE was now feeling an erection starting to form. HE ignored it as she now set the patio table for supper. Sex would have to wait until later.

They enjoyed a nice dinner. BOBBY opened a new bottle of wine. She smiled as he poured her a nice glass. They drank a toast to them. She served dessert. BOBBY was moved by what a great dinner she had put together. She could tell he was pleased. BOBBY poured more wine hoping to get her in a loving mood. She yawned and reached for her cigarettes. HE reached for his lighter and lit her cigarette.

HER lips a lingered on her wine glass She looked at him and smiled and took him by the hand and headed straight for the master bedroom. BOBBY played like he was shy and did not know what to expect. She knew very well what he was up to.

She sat on the edge of the bed as she undressed. Once naked she laid there her long tanned legs so apart he could see the inside of her womanhood. HE was ready for action and bent to kiss her. HE tossed his shirt onto the big leather chair. She took her position as he entered her gently and they made passionate love until both of them were exhausted. They finaly rested and took a cigarette break and had more wine.

The evening wore on. BY ten p/m she had passed out from the wine. HE left her on the bed naked as a jaybird and took a shower trying to recompose himself from all the sex activity. She wore him down some, not that he was complaining but it had been a long day and he needed sleep more than more sex.

HE lit a cigarette just as his cell phone rang. HE grabbed his phone quickly looking at the incoming call number realizing it was from his security at his plant. The guard reported to BOBBY that someone had broken into his business office and they caught the individual on his way out. IT turned out the thief was a former employee of the factory. BOBBY was glad the culprit had been caught. HE hung up the phone and woke ADRIANA told her what the call was about. BObby forced a smile, then grabbed his cigarettes, lit one and leaned back on the over sized leather chair.

ADRIANA sat there on the ottoman totaly naked. She sipped her glass of wine but really what she wanted was to be put in bondage and screwed until the sun came up. HER pussy was real hot and she wanted action and expected it now. HE sensed her needs but finished his wine and cigarette first. HE figured the longer she was kept waiting the better she'd put out.

ADRIANA wanted action, not games and so figured she'd be the agressor. She danced about swaying her boobs, shaking her ass and touching her pussy getting him aroused as best she could. BOBBY loved every minute of it. BOBBY could not believe how big and hairy her pussy was considering she is only about 5 ft. 2" tall. Plus she had tits like a sixteen year old gal. BOBBY loved looking at her. HE now was so aroused he made his move tackling her onto the bed and then spreading her long tanned legs with ease. She kissed him with great compassion, her tongue going deep in his mouth. BOBBY had a hard time keeping up with her. She knew very well how to turn a man on and convince him that she was indeed his sex godess.

They had sex for quite a while until exhaustion set in. BOBBY lit a cigarette. She rolled over looking innocent but she was looking for more sex. She was far from done. She felt she needed at least three more climaxes. She was in heat like a cat. HE fingered her for a while trying to get her to climax but as hard as she tried it did not work out. She had to get laid and that was that. ADRIANA was like a out of control fire seeking sex to put out the flames of love hunger. BOBBY was the guy to satisfy her desires. Their sex lives sizzled. They were definetly soul mates.

One day in the future no doubt she'd become MRS. BOBBY EDWARDS. BOBBY adored her and she adored him as well. They had a chemistry between them that worked. BOBBY was unlike his brother BLAKE.

When it came to women BOBBY chose his very carefuly. HE was a shrewed person, very fussy not the run of the mill guy. Someday maybe he would make a decision to marry some chick but right now he was a man in his twenties getting as much out of life as the world could provide. HE was content with his life at least at the moment. She was an important part of his life. HE had found the perfect woman so he thought.

AN hour or so had past. BOBBY poured two glasses of wine for them and sat down next to her. HE took her right hand in his and kissed it gently and then french kissed her turning her on almost instantly. HE massaged her naked breasts, looked at her closely and suddenly desire for sex was in high gear. She was still wet from the prior sex they had shared. She opened her legs as wide as she could allowing him a real wet entrance to her vagina. HE was ready to shoot off but held back for now. She planned to get her share of sperm whenever she could get him to let it loose. She was a woman with a high caliber need for sex. HE was the man who would satisfy her needs. They were perfect for each other. HE was extremely happy and felt he met his soul mate and their relationship would indeed last forever.

The next morning ADRIANA was up early. She showered and dressed and headed for the kitchen to make breakfast for her and BOBBY. HE was still asleep so she had plenty of time to put a nice breakfast together.

HE was washed out do to screwing her all night but she felt great and sex was invigorating for her man wanted and needed. She wasn't bashful and asked how long his penis was. HE hesitated laughing at her wondering what in the hell she wanted to know that for. She now coaxed him so much that he blurted out that he had a ten inch long one and asked her why did it matter. She replied the longer the better for her. HE ignored her reply. She grabbed his hand and placed it on her belly. BOBBY looked closely at her hairy bush. HE could not believe how thick her black hair was that covered that part he wanted so badly again.

HE rolled her over on her stomach, parted her legs and jammed his throbbing cock into her waiting vagina. She cried out in pain for a moment then moved around getting a better fit. After a while she had multiple orgasms that sent her over the edge of reality. She never could get enough of BOBBYS'throbbing manhood. She loved the thickness of it as he shoved it inside her buttocks. She looked forward to him washing up so she could give him a well deserved blow job. She wasn't shy thats' for sure. She loved oral sex, it turned her on. She especialy loved it when a guy licked her until she climaxed. She ran hot most of the time. BOBBY had no complaints for he was getting his share of hot pussy daily.

BOBBY wondered why she was so sexual. HE never met a woman like her before. HE figured her former husband did not perform well. The EDWARDS boys never had a problem satisfying a beautiful woman. HE learned quickly what she expected in bed for he never wanted to disappoint her ever. She always tried to keep BOBBY happy and kept the bedroom antics new and exciting. After all sex was the important part of the relationship. They both worked hard at satisfying each other on a sexual level. After an exhausting workout they rested. IT was well after two a/m so they needed to get some sleep. BOBBY had a early board meeting and she had an appointment too.

The morning showed itself quickly. The sun peeked through the thin sheer drapes of the lavious bedroom just as the alarm clock set off. BOBBY jumped up quickly and headed for the shower. ADRIANA rolled her nude body over and went back to sleep. She was still tired from the sex capades of the night. BOBBY felt refreshed, renewed, rejuvinated.

BOBBY dressed, drank a quick coffee, took his appointment book from the dresser and headed outside to his car. IN minutes he was down on the main road. Traffic was not bad at this early hour. HE had a meeting with the board of directors at nine sharp and at three p/m he had a meeting with another soap companies c.e.o. and staff to discuss a merge or total buy out of their company for millions of dollars of dollars. BOBBY was prepared to make an offer.

HE wasn't worried in regards to bidding on the competition. Money was no problem. The problem was to get these guys to sell out. HE was ready to take over the small company. HE was smart like his brother BLAKE was on how to wheel and deal. They just knew how to make money. They were very well educated in the world of finance, both guys holding a masters' degree in finance. Money makes money.

BOBBY arrived at the company headquarters. HE pulled into the c.e.o. parking space, grabbed his attache case and headed inside. The front office was busy with multiple phones ringing, security checking on visitors, secrataries typing and answering the phones as BOBBY headed for thc clevator to the third floor board room. HE was a bit nervous as always meeting with his board of directors. HE took a deep breath as he pulled open the meeting room door. The board of directors stood up as he entered the lavious room. BOBBYS' chair was dead center as always and he asked everyone to be seated so the meeting could begin.

The staff served coffee and pastries as the agenda started. The board opened with the notes of the last meeting. BOBBY had ordered an internal audit of all financial records and he turned the meeting over to his attorney who also was a. c. p. a. The figures were impressive at least BOBBY thought so. The possible merger with a smaller soap company was a possibility. IT wa also possible for BOBBYs'company EDWARDS SOAPs would buy it outright making EDWARDS'SOAPS a leader in the industry. BOBBY called for a review of all data and reports and set a final date to decide upon the purchase at the next meeting. After several other items discussed the meeting was now adjourned.

BOBBY grabbed his attache case and headed for his office. HE spoke some quick orders with his secretary and got on the phone with ADRIANA and made dinner plans for that evening. She was excited and horny as well. BOBBY told her he loved her and hung up.

ADRIANA filled her wine glass for the second time. Drinking was her way to escape reality at times. Once in a while she'd think about her dead husband and got depressed a bit and turn to a bottle of wine for comfort. She'd be an alcoholic one day at the rate she put wine away. BOBBY never saw the danger in her consumption of the expensive wines he kept chilled in his wine cellar. Plus he loved her to much to make an issue from it after all his other gals drank heavy so this was nothing he had not dealt with before. BUT ADRIANA was special though, not like the others. She was not only a great sex partner but she was his chosen soul mate. HE had slept with her on their third date and he had never forgot the first time he saw her naked. She had the body of a young cheer leader. She could screw three times a day and still want more. BOBBY was thrilled having a sexualy active lady-what man would not be?

With his days activities complete he headed home to his lover ADRIANA. She was waiting patiently anxious to have a quickie as soon as he arrived. She laid on the water bed in her white terry robe completely nude underneath, her body in heat anxious to take him inside of her. She lit a cigarette and she poured another glass of wine. BY the time BOBBY would arrive she'd be drunk.

BOBBY had made reservations in BEVERLY HILLS. She'd have to sober up or they would have to cancel their plans. She heard a car drive up. BOBBY had arrived. She ran to the door and wrapped herself around him getting his attention immediately. BOBBY was surprised. HE let go of her quickly and seemed a little angry that she had been drinking heavy. She smiled at him as she dropped her robe to the floor exposing her nudity. She pulled him into the bedroom anticipating a love making session. BOBBY grabbed her by the wrists and moved her aside. HE was pissed she could see it in his eyes.

HE called her a drunk. She cried and then apologized. HE apologized. They kissed softly then the fireworks of sex started. HE undressed quickly as she positioned herself ready for action. She now spread her legs wide open showing her wetness awaiting his big cock for her big vagina. She pulled him down with rapid movement on top of her parting long legs in anticipation of another lustful time. HE took her as quick as he could fit himself inside her hot waiting body. She climaxed so quickly not holding back anymore. She was just getting started. HE was in for a sexual ride he'd never forget anytime soon. HER body was hot as a fire. She wanted him inside her deeper yet if it was at all possible. She made moves like a teenage virgin having sex for the first time ever.

BOBBY was anxious to get done with it. HE wanted to shower and get ready to go out to dinner. SEX tonight could wait for a while later. She wanted attention and wanted it now with no delays. BOBBY had no choice but to give her what she wanted. HE wasn't really in the mood for sex. HE gave into her pretending to be caught up in the moment. After several climaxes ADRIANA was somewhat satisfied and BOBBY headed for the shower. She laid there satisfied puffing on her cigarette and in between sipping her wine again.

Meanwhile BObby showered, hinted for her to shower which after dropping her half filled glass all over the PERSIAN rug.

She headed into the bathroom. She was getting annoying now to BOBBY. HE was not one to start to argue but he was getting pissed off with her drinking and carrying on but it really pissed him off if a woman was drunk a lot. ADRIANA didn't care to curb her taste for booze after all she still gave him pussy even when she was a little looped from to much wine.

BOOBY never turned down sex of any kind. She could satisfy him no matter what she drank or how much she drank. BOBBY looked at the clock. IT was already close to seven p/m. Finaly she was ready and it seemed the shower had helped shake that drunken feeling.

BOBBY was dressed in his blue PIERE CARDIN blazer, white shirt, white boat shoes looking as chipper now as he can be. ADRIANA had dressed in a white ruffled blouse, white slacks and white heels by PRADA. They looked great together almost like two celebrities in love. Hand and hand they headed out to the car.

The sun was going down over MALIBU as they took the PACIFIC COAST HIGHWAY and headed west. ADRIANA had no idea where he had made reservations. HE kept it a secret so as to really surprise her. After an hour or so of driving BOBBY pulled the MERCEDES into a looped parking lot up on a hill over looking a romantic view of the city. She had never been there before. BOBBY knew of "SIR DAVIDS'STEAK HOUSE" by the ocean which had a great reputation of being the best server of filet mignon within the region. BOBBY had indeed surprised her.

A valet took the car and parked it. The front of the place was clustered with rose bushes and white trellises of all kinds of flowers. THE place over looked the ocean and the interior was just gorgeous with large white tables each with a spray of flowers in a TIFFANY vase. Scattered white leather booths added a nice touch along with lighting that enhanced the beautiful decor of the days of medieval times of merry old ENGLAND. The place was like stepping into a magic world—a fantasy world so breath taking, so unlike anything she had ever seen.

BOBBY smiled as the hostess showed them to their private table out on the remote patio deck exclusively a setting restricted to known movie stars, business tycoons and other millionaires. ADRIANA was impressed for sure. She felt like a princess in a book opened to her favorite fairy tale when she was just a girl.

BOBBY and her were seated and a bottle of wine compliments of the owner was brought to their table. BOBBY was well known where ever he went and people fussed around him as if he were the president. BOBBY lit a cigarette as the waitress handed them the velvet lined menues. ADRIANA reached for his hand, the excitement in her large hazel colored eyes showed the happiness that she endured. BOBBY caressed her warm finger tips, her perfume drifted towards him, her beautiful mouth showing a million dollar smile. This place had deeply moved her emotions.

The waiter dressed as a court jester took their order. The hostess was dressed like a queen out of a childs' fairytale. The decor was based on merry ole ENGLAND. This place certainly had the atmosphere for an unusal setting for dining. ADRIANA was fascinated by it and BOBBY was pleased.

IN a short while their two steak dinners were brought to the table. A large tossed CAESAR SALAD with bread sticks seemed to top off the meal. BOBBY ordered an expensive bottle of wine. The waiter opened the wine and poured them each a glass of red wine that really rounded out the dinner. The wine smelled sweet and its' taste was like no other they had ever had before. They made small talk over dinner.

The night had a beautiful setting of warm air as the ocean caressed the shore line in the glittering moonlight. IT was the tail end of JULY just so perfect for dining outside.

AS the evening wore on BOBBY and ADRIANA ordered dessert. The waiter poured coffee and sat down in front of them imported french chocalate cakes covered in heavy chocalate syrup and a scoop of chocalate ice cream in a crystal small bowl. ADRIANA smiled as she fed BOBBY a taste of the cake. BOBBY bit into the cake like a kid at a party. After a dinner that had lasted three hours the couple left and headed up the coast towards his MALIBU house.

They talked a little as he drove along the beach. They both agreed that the dinner was superb. ALL in all it had been a great day. The night air was unusualy cool and the moon cast a fraction of the light it seemed than usual. There was a mild breeze now that it was approaching eleven p/m. BOBBY was glad they took the MERCEDES and not the red CADILAC convertible. HE put on the heater on low to ward off a chill that seemed to occur. She fell asleep while BOBBY drove along THE PACIFIC COAST HIGHWAY. BOBBY looked over at her and the way she looked at the moment brought back the visions of how they had met that SPRING day at the shopping mall. HE smiled remembering he nearly knocked her over not watching where he was walking. HE picked up her bags that were knocked to the floor and offered to buy her lunch for being so stupid and to his surprise she had indeed accepted his offer. IT seemed so long ago that they met at the CENTURY CITY MALL. HE smiled as he took the exit leading out to his place

She hadn't stirred a bit. BOBBY did not want to wake her for real soon they'd be home at his beach house. AN hour or so had passed and now BOBBY was just pulling into his driveway. HE shut off the engine and spoke her name in a whisper then a bit louder finaly she opened her eyes realizing they were home. She needed assistance to get out of the car so BOBBY came around on the passenger side to assist herShe was still a bit sleepy. She needed him to hold her arm as she made her way up the wrought iron trimmed staircase. She removed her shoes at the door so not to dirty the pure white rug that went from the foyer throughout the living room to the guest bedroom as well as the master bedroom.

BOBBY liked the white rug because it highlighted the black leather furniture as well as the white lamps with their blue lamp shades. HE removed his western boots in the foyer where a mat was placed so as to keep the area clean.

BOBBY lit a cigarette then poured them a chilled glass of wine each. She called for a toast to their relationship. Their glasses touched. HE leaned forward towards her and kissed her. They talked about how great dinner was and that it was nice to get out of the house for a change. She sure enjoyed a night out and even though they had hired a part time cook ADRIANA loved cooking for him. She wanted to show him that she was wife material not just a bed partner when he needed sex. BOBBY adored her wheter she could cook or not wasn't a issue after all they had hired RITA GOMEZ to cook part time so no big deal.

BOBBY showered while she watched THE FOOD CHANNEL. ADRIANA just loved the food channel cooks. IT put excitement into her day as she learned the tricks to cooking.

BOBBY dressed now in his white terry robe entered the bedroom. The smell of his very expensive cologne filled the room with a nice hint of a well known brand fragrance. IT was time for her to shower. She slipped out of her blouse and her black laced bra. She dropped her slacks onto the floor and now took off her black laced panties exposing her perfectly trimmed pussy. BOBBY was not surprised by her teasing. HE knew he was in for a rough ride of hot sex that night her smile told the whole story. HE knew the signs that told him she was in a horny mood. She finished her shower and returned to the bedroom in a black negligee that gave him all the inspiration he needed to get in the mood for some steamy sex.

She sat down next to him, lit a cigarette and sipped at her wine knowing very well what was on her mind. She was ready for action. ADRIANA dropped her white silk robe to the floor. She stood there stark naked, her large breasts anxious to be sucked with their red nipples fully erect waiting for BOBBY to give her what she craved. HE lit a cigarette, poured two more glasses of chilled wine for them handed one to her as he grabbed her ass with one hand. She groaned as he rubbed the crack of her buttocks. HER moaning warned him that she was ready now. HE was getting a good stiff erection and she reached for his penis stroking it faster and faster. HEwas ready to shoot off. She wanted him inside her now. She spread her legs wide and with her right hand guided his penis to her opening. She was wet, ready to climax

She was always hot. Even as a teen she did tricks for all kinds of guys never satisfying herself 100%. She loved sex since she was twelve years old and by the age of fiftheen had three abortions. Now she was an adult with a sexual appetite that was out of control. HE was ready to shoot his load and in a brief moment he let loose driving her over the edge as she placed her hand on his balls.

HE was surely satisfied as they broke loose and he lit an expensive cigar. HE was beat at least for now. HE needed a breather. IF he wanted more sex she'd turn on in no time at all. She was far from bashful. She seemed hot all the time like her body and mind demanded an abundance of sex. She was a middle aged woman but had the endurance of a teenage gal. She could have sex until exhausation set in. She loved sex more than anything. IT made her feel alive. BOBBY wasn't complaining at all.

IT was close to three a/m as he poured two chilled glasses of wine. Wine relaxed him. She liked wine too. HE lit a cigarette and leaned back on the bed giving her a gaze at her lucious naked body with only one thing on his mind. She sat at the edge of the bed, her large breasts just hanging needing to be caressed. She was ready once more and BOBBY was well aware but he needed to rest a bit before trying to give her a stiff cock that would satisfy her pussy. She never seemed to get tired and had an endless energy level.

BOBBY caught on to her message. HErolled over and was ready to take her on. She slid into position teasing him in her own way, making him wait for the treasure he desired from her. IN seconds they were in a compromising position. She opened her legs grabbed his cock and shoved it inside her. IN seconds it seemed she was sceaming as loud as she could as her climax built up to its'peak. BOBBY was going to ride her as hard as he could which she loved. Finaly they reached their orgasmsand both of them laid there purely exhausted.

BOBBY went into the bar in the living room and filled two chilled glasses with the best wine money could buy. BOBBY had bottles of wine worth as much as a new CADILAC fully loaded. HE had great taste in wine, besides great taste in beautiful women. HE always had the best things life could offer. After his brother BLAKES' death BOBBY inherited all of BLAKES' estate worth billions. HE would never hurt for money. The family had old money they never spent as of yet, so he had the world by the ass.

They made plans to fly out to NEW YORK CITY. BOBBY had a business venture there. HE was going to bid on another soap company worth millions. HE was invited to a a special seminar through their lawyers. HIS lawyers had planned to meet him there. The hotel had their reservations set up. BOBBY had set up with the HILTON hotels. BOBBY had rented a full luxury suite for them. IT will be the business deals first then fun time in NEW YORK CITY for as long as they wanted for BOBBYS' calendar was freed up. They would dine at the best places and she could go on a great shopping spree. She loved shopping. She went a lot out to RODEO DRIVE to shop for clothes and purses. SHE had inherited millions from her first husbands'life insurance. Plus she was born into a rich family who owned oil fields and sold oil to the giants in the business.

ADRIANA could shop anywhere her heart desired. HER credit cards had no limits. HER checking account had no boundaries. She had the world by the ass just like BOBBY. BOBBY and her were living life to the max.

They decided to pack their suitcases the next day and take an earlier flight towards the end of the week. She was excited for this was his first trip into NEW YORK CITY. BOBBY had been there several times and knew his way around. Plus he used a limo service where ever he went to escort he and his lady for whatever choices they made. Money wasn't a problem for BOBBY was left millions in a will from his brother BLAKE and the soap company he owned broke well over a billion dollars in sales in just the first six months of the current year.

Life was good and BOBBY had it all in the palm of his hands. ADRIANA was so excited to be going into NEW YORK CITY, the stores, the live plays-dining in the most exclusive places and being with one of the richest guys in NORTH AMERICA was the ultimate according to her very own words. She was treated like a princess and all she had to do is give him pussy whenever he wanted it wheter or not she was in the mood did not matter to him. HE took whatever he wanted, whenever he wanted from her. She lived a life of pure luxury that any woman would die for. She was treated fairly and then some. She screwed him, kept him happyand was given the world at her finger tips. From fur coats, to diamond rings, to luxury cars, to the best clothing and shoes that the world offered and it of course was all for her in return for affection real or not. BOBBYS' love for her was like a out of control roller coaster ride. HE wanted sex in a moments'noticeand she obliged him.

With the packing all done ADRIANA cooked dinner. She charcoaled on the grills two big steaks, a few ears of corn and tossed a nice salad fit for a king. She was quite a cook. AT a young age as she attended a culinary school in L/A. She was not a chef but could put out meals as good as if not better than those folks now getting the glamour spot on cable food shows. She pleased BOBBY with her meals that's all that mattered.

She fussed about with her meal prep. She had wanted to make sure BOBBY was happy with her cooking skills aas well as her sexual games.

Dinner went well. BOBBY opened a bottle of FRENCH wine. HE loved wines and his wine cellar was packed just about every kind of wine anyone would love to taste. HE spent thousands a year on imported wines and beers. HE enjoyed the best and thought hey that is what money is for to enjoy the fine things life has to offer. ADRIANA was spoiled by her lover. She always had the best life can offer after all she lived with a very rich man and one day to be her husband she figured. IT was just a matter of time she figured that he'd propose to her. Only time would tell.

IT was after nine p/m when BOBBY decided he wanted dessert. She had surprised him with a two layer strawberry whip cream cake. She served him a piece and sat next to him. She was content that her dinner prep and dessert had satisfied the guy she was so deeply in love with. BOBBY leaned close to her and kissed her gently on the cheek. She smiled as she reached for her chilled glass of wine.

IT was reaching close to ten p/m and BOBBY had to check his sports channel to see how the YANKEES were doing. HE was a baseball fan for years and attended many games with his rich dad as a kid growing up in the heart of NEW YORK CITY. His father had owned several small businesses at the time in MANHATTAN.

The family lived in a mansion on the outskirts of NEW YORK and owned another mansion in the city of GREENWICH, CONNECTICUT at the time. IT was true BOBBYS' father came from money so the family hadn't used up the old money as of yet. Over the years different many relatives had handed down wealth to one another. The family had more money than the CATHOLIC CHURCHES.

Finaly midnight rolled around and it was time to wind down-and get ready for the bedroom games only adults can play. She undid her white blouse and slipped out of her bra quickly and her breasts dangled nicely in front of BOBBY which he turned on almost in a heart beat. Then she slid off her slacks tossed them on a chair and dropped her black laced panties onto the rug, then spread her legs widely for BOBBY to enter her without a problem. BOBBY was anxious now with burning desire for her. IN no time at all she took a sitting position lining up perfect with his hard penis which she just could not get enough of. She had boundless sexual energy.

ADRIANA wanted her usual share of mutiple orgasms. She was determined always to get her self satisfied but for sure wanted to also satisfy him—the man who had her heart right from the begining of their affair. She could get him off with very little effort. Their lovemaking went for well over two hours with very little rest in between. They were like two college kids caught up in the moment on SPRING break. Finaly they broke away from each other. BOBBY headed for the bathroom, then to the bar to get two chilled glasses of a FRENCH wine

She called for a toast to their relationship. Their glasses tingled. BOBBY lit one of his imported cigars he use to order from a company in CANADA. HE always had expensive taste in whatever he bought after all he could well afford it. She was being spoiled by BOBBY. Whatever her heart desired he'd buy for her. Money was so plentiful. HE had several bank accounts, stock in certain companies and cash always in his wallet to play with any way he'd like. HE had life by the ass and enjoyed all the world could offer at any given moment. His brother BLAKE was the same way.

These guys were the mega money makers. They came from a very rich family which for generations made millions in oil rigging, auto manufacturing and other companies. The money rolled in from all directions. These guys were in the league with the KENNEDYS, the VANDERBILTS and all the rest of the rich dogs. They had so much money that at any given time they'd have to estimate what their worth was—they really did not know how much they had at any given point in time.

IT was nearing three a/m when they finaly got to bed. She wanted more sex. BOBBY was tired but she was insisting and reached over and grabbed him. She pulled him on top of her and in no time he was inside her, riding her to her next climax.

She turned him every way but loose. She was hot. HE was in for a rough and tough ride because she wanted more than he could deliver at the moment. She wasn't shy.

She was at the point when she wanted him and that was that. She started climaxing before he could come even a little. She was gyrating like an animal in heat. Finaly she scratched his back with her nails like a loose lunatic. She took a deep breath and reached an orgasm that took her over the edge. IT was a night he would never forget.

A hour or so later they rested, drank some wine, smoked a joint to relax. BOBBY was now sweaty and exhausted. She was satisfied from all the sex but wanted more sex before she called it a night. She had quite a sexual appetite at times. For a middle aged woman she could show a guy a real good time in bed guaranteed no boredom with her between the sheets. BOBBY glanced at her sweating body. HE knew very well she wasn't quitting yet. She had a little spark left and was ready to burst into a flaming sex godess.

She could take a man pleasantly to heaven without him dying. She knew everyway to please a guyand was not bashful to try anything new if asked by her partner. Nothing bashful about her she declared when making love. They made love for about another hour and quit to enjoy more chilled wine and a cigarette to relax with. HE poured them some expensive wine.

They talked about the trip to NEW YORK CITY. She was more excited than BOBBY was. HE had becn there numerous times but this was a first for her. All she could think about is the retail stores, great places to eat and seeing the sights and just having fun. After all being a rich mans' babe paid off in dividends even if it meant that you had to sleep with him and satisfy all of his sexual desires. She would have to pack her suitcase in the next day or so because they'd leave by that FRIDAY. She would plan out an itinarary for both of them. She loved making plans when they traveled wheter for business for him or just a pleasure trip. She loved to travel, seeing new places, meeting BOBBYS' rich friends, going out to fancy places for dinner and staying in the most expensive hotels is a double suite.

She was living the life of a princess, a godess, a queen. The next few days passed quickly with BOBBY at several meetings, packing for the trip, etc. Finaly FRIDAY arrived.

BOBBY and ADRIANA were up at four a/m. HIS private limo driver would arrive there at five a/m and they'd head out to the airport for a six thirty a/m flight. ADRIANA was all excited. They showered, dressed, ate a good breakfast and sat in the living room relaxing until JAX his driver showed up. They chatted about NEW YORK CITY and how nice the summer weather would be now. She lit a cigarette, trying to relax a bit.

BOBBY now reviewed the airline tickets and tucked them into his sport jacket pocket. They were both getting anxious as they waited patiently. IT was close to five when they heard the limo pull up on the immense driveway. BOBBY now grabbed a couple of suitcases as JAX rang the bell. BOBBY let him in and now with JAXS' assistance the men loaded the suitcases into the trunk of the limo.

IN no time the black stretch limo pulled out of the driveway and got onto the open road heading for L. A. X. airport. JAX would pick up the freeway and they'd arrive just in time for their flight at AMERICAN AIRLINES. BOBBY used this airline all the time because he owned a considerable amount of stock in it. HE also for private flights had his own piloted lear jetbased at another airport.

HE had the cash flow to keep his living at the top like the saying goes. ADRIANA was impressed by BOBBYS' lifestyle. HEwas rich and famous but a humble guy.

They arrived at the airport on schedule. IT was a one hour wait for their flight. JAX wished them a safe trip as BOBBY placed a hundred dollar bill into his hand. JAX smiled and drove off heading back to the estate. The skycap took their bags as they headed to the nearest bar for a pick up drink of some sort. With a couple of drinks consumed it was time to board the aircraft. They went to the gate and boarded the aircraft. ADRIANA was so excited. She could not wait to get to NEW YORK CITY, The city lights, big skyscrapers, BROADWAY, the retail storesand of course CENTRAL PARK.

Their seats were in the more expensive area of the plane, after all he is BOBBY EDWARDS-little brother of BLAKE EDWARDS very wealthy and expected to be treated with as much respect as you could muster up. HE after all was BOBBY EDWARDS C.e.o. OF at the time the largest industrial soap company in the U.S.A. and was in the mist of buying the competition in WEST GERMANY. Everywhere he had ever gone in this country people would indeed recognize him. HE was a celebrity in a way, a business tycoon like DONALD TRUMP. HEwas a high flyer, rich, handsome, intelligent business man.

The flight would last five hours, then land at J. F. K. airport. They ate a light lunch and had a few drinks. BOBBY always flew first class after all he could afford it. His next flight would be in a month or so to WEST GERMANY to close the business deal. HE would travel then using his private jet and his personal pilot. ADRIANA would attend this meeting as his personal consultant. HIS jet had a full bath, bedroom and all the comforts of home, after all he could very well afford this lifestyle. BOBBY enjoyed the attention he recieved with the media and the big business tycoons that were jet setters.

The jet pilot announced landing would be within fiftheen minutes or so. BOBBY reached up into the overhead compartment for her hand held suitcase. She stood up and had to stretch. The plane landed softly and the pilot brought it nicely up to the gate of departure. BOBBY and ADRIANA were some of the first to depart. The crowd moved along in an orderly manner.

Instead of going to get their belongings BOBBY insisted on dining at the small eatery tucked away in a corner. HE had eaten there a few times before and knew the ITALIAN owners. MARIO one of the owners spotted BOBBY and sent a bottle of his best wine to his old friend. MARIO waited a few minutes then he headed for BOBBYS' table. BOBBY stood up and hugged his friend who he hadn't seen in a long while. BOBBY introduced ADRIANA and she smiled graciously at MARIO. MARIO was glad to see BOBBY for it had been a good year since BOBBY had been in NEW YORK. MARIO opened the wine and poured his guests each a glass. BOBBY and MARIO talked about business deals.

BOBBY talked about opening a chain of ITALIAN EATERIES and have MARIO handle all of as the territory manager. The men would talk again in the future about this deal. BOBBY wanted this deal so badly and had the cash flow so money wasn't an issue just time was his worst enemy, because of so many other commitments. BOBBY handed MARIO his business card and told him to e-mail him all the info about the franchises so that he could review it at his leisure. BOBBY wanted this deal so he could be more deversified in investments. HIS brother BLAKE when he was c.e.o did things a lot differently. BOBBY was out to show his family just how smart he was.

BOBBY and Adriana said quick goodbyes as they headed out to pick up their luggage and meet their limo driver who would take them to their hotel in lower MANHATTAN. IT seemed in no time flat their limo driver was pulling up to the curb. After loading their suitcases they drove off heading for the hotel in lower MANHATTAN. BOBBY poured them a drink from his small refrigerator bar. ADRIANA smiled she loved this good lifestyle he had provided for her. The ride seemed to had ended sooner than expected. The driver pulled up to the curb at the side entrance of the hotel. The limo driver opened the doors for them and reached into the trunk to get suitcases for his boss. The hotel bus man placed the suitcases on a rolling truck and rolled the unit into the front lobby.

The limo driver was tipped very well by BOBBY and left for the day. ADRIANA and BOBBY checked in. Their adjoining suites were ready. They took the elevator to the twentitieth floor. IT was a express elevator to their floor. IT was an express elevator ride and in no time the bellhop opened the door to the adjoining suites. HE tipped the bellhop twenty bucks and now went to the main bar in the corner of the room. HE grabbed two chilled glasses from the refrigerator and a bottle of FRENCH wine from the rack, popped the cork, poured two drinks and handed one to her calling for a toast at the same time. Their glasses clinked and she smiled again feeling like a fairytale princess.

Now all she needed was some hot sex which lately they have not had due to BOBBYS' busy lifestyle and his company and all. She suggested they'd shower together put some excitement in their lives for sure. She removed her blouse, then her black laced bra, then her bluejeans, then her laced panties exposing now all her hidden assets which got his attention. BOBBY was jet lagged but under these circumstances he would rise to the occassion. She was hot to the touch like a flaming inferno. HER thighs widened as she took him deep inside her. She screamed for more as she reached climax. almost instantly because she was a horny bitch.

She was now like a cat in heat of the night. BOBBY kissed her breasts as she screamed for him to go deeper as she clawed his back to hell with her long fingernails. She was so turned on that there was no way to turn her off. She was a hot bitch and that was the bottom line. She wanted to be satisfied.

She knew how to bring the best sex wise out of her man. She could make love in so many ways beyond BOBBYS' imagination for sure. BOBBY was crazy about her but wasn't sure he was ready for marriage yet. HE had never been married.

Here they were in NEW YORK CITY making love like it was their first time. They finaly rested after a good hour of sexual bliss. HE was exhausted from her antics which drained him but he had no complaints after all she satisfied his needs alright. She knew how to sexualy satisfy her man. She could make her body do all kinds of tricks. She had had a lot of experience with men from as early as twelve years old and had learned the ropes. AT twelve she was already well developed and boasted that she had a 34c boob size. She strutted her stuff and got lots of attention from all comers. She made a quick buck doing tricks for older guys. HER mother had put her on birth control pills from an early age knowing her daughter was having sexual contact with different guys.

She also got into threesomes, sometimes with men and sometimes with women. She was a bi-sexual in those days but later prefered men for they really got her off the way she needed to get off.

BOBBY now poured two more glasses of wine and then lit a cigarette trying to relax. IT had been a long day already and being with ADRIANA could very well make it a long night as well. She never seemed to run out of energy. She certainly knew how to satisfy BOBBY. She gave herself to him totaly. BOBBY cherished her.

The next morning arrived. BOBBY was in the shower getting ready for his day. ADRIANA was asleep yet. BOBBY had no meetings slated so he and she could spend a nice day in NEW YORK CITY. HE did not want to wake her at least not now.

HE finished his shower, dressed and headed for the kitchen to make his coffee. HE set his coffee pot up, lit a cigarette and took out a map of MANHATTAN. HE was planning a sightseeing tour for them. This would be a special day for both of them especialy her who had never seen NEW YORK CITY before. HE was very familiar with NEW YORK. HE had been there for meetings for his company a few times. NEW YORK CITY was new to ADRIANA and she was anxious to explore it. BOBBY wanted to get to see a YANKEE game. ADRIANA liked baseball so a trip out to the stadium would be great

BOBBY drank his coffee and had a cigar. IN a short time ADRIANA came out to the room wearing her bathrobe looking a little messy but her pretty smile perked things up as she leaned forward to kiss him good morning. She headed for the shower and in a short while was dressed ready to go. BOBBY grabbed the door key and they headed to the elevator. AT the lobby BOBBY and ADRIANA stepped outside into the summer sunlight and hailed a taxi. BOBBY told the driver to head to his most favorite diner on BROADWAY. HE figured they'd get breakfast then head out onto the magical BROADWAY and enjoy their first day in the city.

ADRIANA was happy and curious as she entered the diner with BOBBY. She was now looking out the diner window at the crowds as they moved about and the traffic noises got her attention. She felt really alive as the excitement of NEW YORK CITY built up.

The waitress took their order and poured two coffees and then came back with two fresh orange juices. IN a short time their food was brought to the table. They made lots of small talk as they ate breakfast. She still watched the crowds outside as people moved about, rushing here and there.

After paying their tab they stepped out to BROADWAY. To ADRIANA the excitement was now building even more so as she gazed into the windows of the stores as the crowd seemed to build even more so. BOBBY took it all in stride for he had seen so much of the city on previous business trips.

AS the morning moved along BOBBY and she went shopping in some of the stores that attracted tourists. ADRIANA was excited as she entered a ladies' clothing store. She was amazed at the selection she found there. She purchased an expensive hand bag and shoes. IT was noon as they headed up the avenue. They stopped and bought pretzels and a drink and sat on a bench enjoying the summer day.

HE had suggested taking a tour bus so as to see some of the highlights of MANHATTAN. Adriana could not believe the sizes of the skyscrapers. This city was so different from being in L/A. She was amazed by the way NEW YORK CITY was so busy, so alive, so wonderful to visit. She shot a lot of film too as the tour bus made its'way along the busy streets. She was falling in love with NEW YORK.

BOBBY held her hand and kissed her as the bus rolled along. She was happy that he had taken her to NEW YORK CITY. She had read lots of books on the city and now it became a reality which thrilled her to no end. She was amazed by how big NEW YORK CITY was and how many people lined the streets. There was so much activity at one time it overwhelmed her.

BOBBY had a meeting the next morning and was meeting with buyers of the competition. HE wanted to get the specifics of how much they wanted to be bought out as a subsidiary for his corperation. HE figured he'd place a bid on it and go from there. Money wasn't an issue.

BOBBY smiled as he reached for his pack of cigarettes. He lit one, offered her one and helped light hers. They found a bench and sat down for a while. IT had been an exhausting walk since getting off the scenic bus tour. BOBBY looked at the street signs and told her GRAND CENTRAL RAILROAD STATION was two blocks away and that there was a coffee shop there that had fresh pastries that she just had to try tasting. They rested a while then headed to the well known train station.

Within a short time they entered the famed station. Adriana was amazed by its'beauty. HE explained to her that that they had renovated it. She gazed up at the beautiful painted ceiling as the crowds rushed to their trains. She took a deep breath, smiled, grabbed him by the arm and walked briskly along heading to the little coffee place hidden in one of the many corridors. IN a few minutes BOBBY had spotted the place and they walked casualy to the glass case where lots of beautiful hot pastries awaited their attention. The smell of pastries and coffee filled the air so enticing to the human appetite. BOBBY asked for two black coffees and two chocalate eclairs. They walked to a empty bench and sat down. They made a lot of small talk. They sipped at their coffee and ate at their eclaires. ADRIANA loved the eclair. HE finished his as they watched the crowd move quickly to their waiting trains. The place was crowded. After finishing their coffee they headed outside to the main avenue to pursue more shopping. The crowds thickened as the afternoon headed into evening.

The sun was going down as they shopped more stores. She had her AMERICAN EXPRESS card and was grabbing up as many bargains as she could. Life was great, spending was fun. ITwas all about materialistic things as much as money could buy. BOBBY wanted to buy a real nice dress watch prefered a ROLEX. HE spotted a expensive jewelry store as they crossed over the street and headed inside. ITwas an exquisite shop with so much to choose from. ADRIANA spotted diamond earings and called the lady clerk over. She wanted to try on several styles. Meanwhile BOBBY tried on several stlyes of ROLEXES. IN a short while BOBBY bought a watch and walked over to show it to ADRIANA. She was pleased with his choice. She asked his opinion about the earings and gave his objective opinion and helped her choose the nicest set and gave the clerk a thousand dollars cash for her choice of diamond earings. They left the store pleased with their purchases.

IT was close to dinner time now as they headed up FIFTH AVENUE. BOBBY hailed a cab and told the driver to head over to TRIBECCA to a restaurant he knew of. They arrived there shortly and they headed inside the lavious restaurant. The waiter sat them at a private table in the back where privacy was provided. BOBBY tipped the waiter as they sat down and reviewed the menues. The prices on the menues were steep but BOBBY never ever worried about cost after all he was quite rich. ADRIANA suggested a salad, baked potatoe and a prime rib well done and cheesecake for a dessert. BOBBY agreed with her suggestions. AS the waiter poured some expensive wine they smiled at each other-then called a toast to their relationship. They sipped their wine and decided on her suggestions and the waiter took their order and hurried to the kitchen.

After a while the waiter brought their food. The waiter filled their glasses with more wine. She hesitated for a moment not knowing what to eat first since everything looked so good. "Something wrong love?" 'he asked her watching her closely. "OH, NO its'just everything looks so good" she replied. "YES the food looks so beautifuly placed on the plate doesn't it?" he commented. "Sure does sweety" she answered. They made small talk as they enjoyed their meals. "This is what life is all about" ADRIANA whispered.

Finaly the meal was finished and the waiter brought the coffee along with the cheesecake. BOBBY had ordered the larger slices for them because she loved cheesecake as much as he did. The cheesecake was topped with cheeries. She was surprised by the size of the slices.

AN hour passed and they paid their tab and headed out to the lobby. BOBBY took out his cell phone and called his limo service who were very prompt in response. The limo arrived in fiftheen minutes. BOBBY told them to return to the hotel. IN a short while they were at the hotel. The driver carried their bags as they made their way to the elevator. BOBBY opened their door and tipped the driver. She lit a cigarette as she dropped into a large leather lounge chair. BOBBY was at their bar pouring two glasses of wine.

IT had been a long day. BOBBY had a meeting the next morning on FIFTH AVENUE to see about a bid on another soap company he was interested in. HE needed to shower, shave, set up his clothes and of course make love to his beautiful partner. She was getting the urge to have sex too. IN a short time she started to undress. She was going to tease him enough to have a hot sex workout. BOBBY eyed her nakedness and started to get horny. IT was time to make his move.

She laid there naked, her heart beating like a drum knowing very well BOBBY was going to deliver what she wanted. HE now had an erection hard as hell and throbbing. IT was the right time alright to slide into position. She spread her long legs, her bush lying there open so he could see inside her. HE grabbed her legs and placed himself inside her getting that nice tight feeling. She gasped for breath and screamed for more. She scratched his back with her finger nails yelling out loud like a cat in heat. She finaly climaxed and dropped from exhaustion. IT was time to relax now. IT was time for a cigarette and a chilled glass of wine

They sat there sipping their wine. Their bodies full of perspiration from the love making session that lasted at least two hours. Exhausted but satisfied for sure.

The next morning seemed to come quickly. BOBBY was up before sunrise. HE had to shower, get on his best dress clothes, have a quick breakfast, also review his speech for the big meeting with another group from the competitive soap company. HE was going to place a bid on the competition no doubt an offer they could not refuse. IF he closed this deal then he'd own several soap companies. HE was on his way to control a high percent of the nations'soap business.

HE made his morning pot of coffee and made toast and had a chilled glass of o. j., he felt confident that he was going to close the deal. HE was a wheeler and dealer and had cold hard cash he could bring to the table. IT wasn't about money but about power and control.

HE headed to the elevators. HE got off on the ground floor where he met his limo driver. They headed outside to the street where the stretch limo was parked. IN a flash they were gone on their way. IT was business as usual.

The traffic was heavy through lower MANHATTAN. They reached the building on FIFTH AVENUE and the limo driver stayed with the car as BOBBY EDWARDS headed into the main office. HE was greeted by a secretary who showed him to the elevators. BOBBY took the elevator to the fifth floor. AS the doors opened he was greeted by NICK CARLSON C.e.o.

and CHIEF FINANCIAL OFFICER who shook his hand and walked with him to the large board room. The meeting was called to order.

BOBBY was introduced and walked to the podium. AS he addressed the audience everone was awaiting his speech. BOBBY spoke very sharply to the crowd explaining the details if a sale occurred. HE answered all of the attendees questions. HE stepped down from the podium with quite a loud applause. BOBBY figured he had made quite an impression. HE smiled as he took his seat and the C.e.o. spoke now giving so vital details to his board members.

The meeting now took a break for coffee. BOBBY made small talk with some of the guys. Everyone seemed friendly enough. AFTER the break the meeting resumed for two hours, then lunch was served. Lunch was served then one more hour of a meeting to tie up loose ends

AT the conclusion BOBBY closed his black attache case, shook hands with the C.e.o. Then headed for the elevator. HE was beat and wanted to get back to his hotel, have some wine and have some sex with ADRIANA who no doubt was ready, willing and able at this point. HE headed to the elevators and soon was in the lobby. His limo driver was at the door to escort him to his hotel.

Traffic had increased ten fold now. ITwas after three p/m as they drove through town. HE was pleased with the outcome of the meeting. From the bar in the back seat he poured a glass of expensive FRENCH wine and made a silent toast to his successful meeting. IT was a good bid to be placed and would know the outcome in a day or so. After a short drive they arrived at his hotel. The limo driver opened the rear door as BOBBY stepped out of the vechile. BOBBY tipped the driver, took his attache case from the seat as rain began to fall…

BOBBY took the elevator to his floor. IN moments he was opening the door to his suite. HE was beat. IT had been a long meeting and he needed to unwind.

ADRIANA called his name from the bedroom, he replied. She walked out to the main room. She was dressed in short-shorts so tight that you could see her womanhood shape. HER blouse was a cute sailor design blue and white in color with minature anchors depicted as its' design. HER tennis sneakers were blue and white. She looked sexy BOBBY grabbed her and kissed her and grabbed her ass at the same time. HE put his hands on the back zipper of her tight white shorts and unzipped them quickly. The shorts dropped to the floor and he scooped her up in his muscular arms and carried her to the bed. BY this time he had an erection throbbing and wanted to put it in her rear end. HE pulled off her black laced panties and opened her long legs gently and placed his penis inside her. She yelped for a moment as she took off her blouse and bra and threw them to the floor. She was ready for action. HE was pretty horny too. HE kissed her wildly as he felt her big breasts with her extended nipples. She now groaned like a wild animal as she scratched his back with her long finger nails.

After a good hour or so of hot sex they took a rest. BOBBY lit a cigar, she lit a joint. BOBBY poured two glasses of wine and they made small talk. The night was young yet. BOBBYS' cell phone rang and went to voicemail. She smiled at him. HE was in no mood to talk on the phone, it had been a long day.

BOBBY turned on the tv. set to find the latest sports channel. She sat there quietly as he listened to the baseball scores for the games the night prior. His team had lost but they were still doing well for the season. HE was happy. She filled their wine glasses again and handed BOBBY HIS. HE smiled as he lit another cigar. BOBBY loved a cigar with his wine

BOBBY sat back in his lounge chair with her now lying nude on the couch. HE would have liked more sex but was in need of rest at least for a while. HE was young but not superman when it came to sex. HE could hang in there but he did have some limitations.

BOBBY decided to shower now for he had a brief meeting with his lawyers in the morning. HE gathered his shower needsand headed into the bathroom. ADRIANA finaly was asleep exhausted from the day. HE was glad she was not going to distract him.

After he showered he went to the closet to set up his suit, shirt, tie and shoes for the morning—then retired to the tv area, lit a cigar and tried to relax now. ADRIANA was still asleep. HE turned on the late night news and sports reports. HE watched tv until one a/m then turned in for the night. She was still asleep so he did not want to disturb her. HE just wanted to get some rest so he'd be good in the morning meeting. This was a important meeting.

Morning seemed to arrive quickly. HEwas up early getting ready to face his day. HE put on a pot of coffee, made toast and had a glass of juice which was his regular deal every morning. IN no time he was ready to head out across town to the building on fifth avenue.

His limo driver was in the lobby as he stepped from the elevator. "GOOD MORNING TO YOU MR. EDWARDS". JOHN the limo driver said as he held the door open leading to the street. "GOOD MORNING JOHN" BOBBY replied. JOHN opened the rear limo door nd BOBBY got in and got comfortable. BOBBY now lit a cigarette as the limo pulled away into traffic. IT was a short ride to the place of the meeting. Finaly they arrived. JOHN opened the door for BOBBY. BOBBY headed into the lavious lobby and walked to the desk. The girl behind the counter flirted with himsome and pointed to the elevators. BOBBY eyed the receptionist noticing her firm breasts and her gorgeous smile. HE pressed the key to the floor he needed. A quick ride and the doors opened to the offices of KEIF ENTERPRISES. HE opened the office door and spoke to the receptionist. THE meeting had not started yet.

BOBBY waited patiently and finaly the meeting was announced. BOBBY walked along with others down the long narrow hallway to a lavious room with an extremely long tablewith leather over stuffed chairs. HE saw his name on a card and took a seat with the others. There were well over two dozen men there. BOBBY sat there quietly wondering when they'd get started. HE was a little nervous today.

The meeting started pretty much on time. The chief c.e.o. TIM FAWLEY started the meeting off. HE talked about his company, the stocks increase along with the splits and his interest in selling off his company due to he wanted to retire and head to FLORIDA. The crowd cheered loudly as he continued. IT was a interesting meeting for sure. BOBBY listened to every word. HE had his speech prepared. HE knew what his offer was going to be. HE wanted that company so as to grow his sales in the northeastern part of the U.S.A.

The company was on the move. This year was going to be his best year yet. His company was making him super rich. HE was on top of the world. HIS company was the leader in the soap industry yet he wanted more wealth, he wanted more progress, he wanted to be the man everyone respected. HE was going to reach his goals for sure.

After the c.e.o. spoke BOBBY got up to the podium. IT was his turn to speak and he was ready to convince the crowd that they as stock holders should consider selling the company to the EDWARDS CORPORATION. IT would be a good fit between their company and BOBBYS'. Everyone stood to gain something the way BOBBY explained it. The crowd applauded as BOBBY continued giving the specifics of the buy out. BOBBY talked for quite a while and finaly concluded his speech. The crowd gave him a standing ovation. The chief c.e.o. shook his hand then BOBBY took his seat again. BOBBY felt energized. HE knew he had made a great impression and had come across well with his offer to purchase this company.

Three hours later the meeting had ended at least the first half of it. IT was time for a nice catered lunch. The guests moved into the luncheon room next door. Everyone smiled at BOBBY and a few shook his hand. HE was proud of himself. HE came, he conquered, he won. This was going to be a signed, sealed deal that day for sure. BOBBY was confident in how the situation had gone.

Lunch went quite well. BOBBY mingled among the guests. BOBBY was accepted it seemed by most. With lunch finished it was back to the room for the rest of the meeting. The head c.e.o. took the mike and spoke for a while about what was covered previously. The crowd applauded. IT seemed the investors were pleased with the sale of the company and everyone was pleased with the bid that BOBBY had made in his offer. BOBBY felt this deal was a steal.

The meeting finaly ended. The c.e.o. told BOBBY he'd have an answer on the offer he made by the next week. BOBBY was disappointed for he wanted to close the deal right now. HE grabbed his attache case and shook hands again with the c.e.o. and headed out the door. HE called his limo driver to come pick him up. HE walked to the elevator deep in thought. HE was a little peeved that he did not close the deal right on the spot.

HE entered the lobby and in a short time his limo driver arrived. HE smiled and told his driver to take him to his hotel. IN a short while they arrived at the hotel.

The limo sped away as BOBBY headed for the elevators. AS he got to his room he took a deep breath. HE lit a cigarette as he opened his door. There stood ADRIANA with two glasses of wine in her hands. She handed one to BOBBY who smiled at first. HE sipped the wine, then kissed her, then related to her about his day. She felt bad for him. HE was annoyed.

HE changed his clothes and showered. HE lit a joint trying to relax. She kept rather quiet knowing he felt hurt to some degree. BOBBY did not like to be kept waiting for an answer when it came to deals in business. After all he is BOBBY EDWARDS and that is the bottom line. HE feels the whole world should be at his beckon call. HE wanted to close the deal. Next week seemed so far off. Some things just don't work in your favor he guessed. Well there was hope for he got a great response from the people who were there which gave him hope of closing the deal in the future. Only time will tell.

Bobby needed some wine to help him relax. She poured a nice chilled glass of wine. HE was so tense from the days' meeting. HE was washed out mentaly. HEwas upset because the c.e.o. did not take the deal right on the spot. BOBBY wanted to buy the company so bad with this purchase he'd have the largest soap producing company in the country. Only time will tell if he'll get it.

The evening wore on. BOBBY now had at least three glasses of wine. HE lit up a joint and passed it to her. She took a drag and passed it back to him. BOBBY was getting a little mellow now. HE also was getting horny too. She was getting in the mood too. She started disrobing. First she tossed her blouse onto the chair, then her bra, then her slacks, then her panties and now stood there naked as a jay bird. BOBBY took notice right away. She waltzed over to him, enticing him as much as she could. IN a moment he was grabbing her big boobs. She was excited already. HE was getting an erection just in time to place it inside her for that is what she wanted.

They had hot sex for well over an hour and then took a breather. BOBBY lit a cigar and relaxed a bit. She was at the bar in the far side of the room pouring two glasses of winewhich they always shared after love making

"Sure is great being in NEW YORK again" BOBBY replied. "I love NEW YORK actualy much better than L/A." She said as she handed him a glass of wine. "Do you really?" he replied. "DO you want me to buy a condo in the city that never sleeps?" he asked her. "MY GOD BOBBY would you?" she asked. "IF you my love really wanted to really be here" he added. "Well actualy I would love to be here but, I'D miss L/A. she quoated. "Well if you ever change your mind I'D have to agree with you that I too love the city" BOBBY added with a smile. She smiled in return.

BOBBY was in the mood for another drink. She poured two more glasses of wine. BOBBY suggested dining out in the eatery in the hotel on the first level. She quickly responded with a yes. They both showered together, sharing a quicky as he shot his load up her rear end and she cried out with pleasure. HE washed her entire body and she washed him all over as well.

They finaly finished showering. They got dressed in casual clothes and headed down to the elevators. When they reached the lobby they walked to the right to MICHAELS'STEAK HOUSE, a gorgeous one of a kind in fine dining in the heart of the city. The waiter sat them at a private table in the east wing. BOBBY ordered a bottle of their best ITALIAN wine. The waiter returned, opened and poured their wine as they viewed the menue. BOBBY knew what he wanted. She figured out hers and they ordered.

They made small talk as they waited for their food. IN a short while the waiter came with their dinners. BOBBY had ordered a ribeye and she another cut of steak along with CAESARS'SALADS. The waiter poured more wine. They chatted about NEW YORK CITY and how they wanted to visit THE STATUE OF LIBERTY. The weather was gorgeous so they figured they'd do as much as possible. This was the kind of day to enjoy anything for both of them NEW YORK CITY certainly was the place to enjoy life. Dinner went well and they toasted their relationship with a glass of wine.

After they had dinner they took a walk along the avenue. The clouds were thick and the sounds of the traffic almost deafining. They stopped at an icecream vendor for a soft icecream cone. GOD life was great and they were here in the greatest city in the U.S.A. They sat on a bench and relaxed from all the walking. She finished her icecream and decided to light up a cigarette. BOBBY lit himself a cigar. They did some small talk and decided to move along and see some sights. ADRIANA loved the skyscrapers. She was amzed by the amount of windows in some of the towering buildings. BOBBY asked her if she missed L/A and what a surprise he got when she said no not at all. They walked hand in hand enjoying the sights as well as watching the people as they migrated across the busy streets. NEW YORK CITY was alive with so much going on like a rush of adrenalin on the move. Hours passed and they were getting tired. IT was time to grab a cab and head back to the hotel.

When they arrived at the hotel it was time to unwind and have a drink. BOBBY went directly to the bar in their room, mixed two drinks, lit a cigarette and sat in the big leather chair. HE was going to relax from a tough day. She sat next to him enjoying her flute glass of wine. They drank a toast to themselves as usual. She wanted sex but he was so tired. She as trying to entice him but it did not work. BOBBY wanted dinner not sex. She was in no mood to worry about dinner. IF they were to have dinner they'd no doubt would have room service or dress up and head downstairs to the beautiful eatery on the first level. They discussed eating and decided on room service by ordering from their personel menues. They ordered two steak dinners with all the trimmings. BOBBY ordered another quart of expensive FRENCH WINE.

IN what seemed like a short time there was a knock on the door. IT was room service with their meals. BOBBY tipped the houseman and they sat down to eat. BOBBY opened the wine and proposed a toast to them as was tradition with them. They again talked about NEW YORK CITY. She loved the city lmost as she loved L/A. NEW YORK was alive, vibrant, exciting and invigerating.

They ate supper, showered and decided to watch a movie on the bedroom tv. She lay next to him cuddled up against him like a house cat. HE lit a cigar and she lit a cigarette. They enjoyed the movie. They later made plans for sightseeing for the next morning.

Morning seemed to have come quickly. The sun peeked through the sheer curtains. The sound of the a/c quietly ran cooling the room. IT was seven a/m and NEW YORK CITY was awake already. ADRIANA was in the shower while BOBBY slept quietly. She applied her makeup and dried herself and then slipped into a tight fitting jeans, white halter top that enhanced her boobs. She slipped into her tennis shoes. She was ready for a day in NEW YORK CITY.

She put on a pot of coffee knowing that BOBBY would no doubt be up soon. She wanted to get an early start but he was still asleep yet. Then shortly she heard the shower running. BOBBY would be looking for his coffee very shortly. She popped the bread into the toaster. She figured a quick bite then head out and spend another day in the city that never sleeps.

BOBBY seemed unusualy quiet. HE was still upset over not closing that other deal out last week. HE was determined to buy out all the small companies and become the largest soap company in the world. HE would follow up on the last deal for sure. HE had to. ITwas the only way he'd wipe out the competition. BOBBY had a quick coffee and got dressed in a hurry. HE wanted to take ADRIANA out to see THE STATUE OF LIBERTY. ITwas a nice SPRING day so he figured why not enjoy it and put business aside for now. HE told her his idea and she highly agreed that would be nice way to spend part of their day in the city. She wanted to see THE EMPIRE STATE as well among other tourist attractions. BOBBY called his limo driver and instructed him to be at their hotel pronto. First he figured they'd eat breakfast at a plush place he knew on BROADWAY, then head out to see the STATUE OF LIBERTY.

They locked their room and headed for the elevators. AS they reached the lobby his limo driver was standing there. The three of them headed outside to the limo. OFF they were to BROADWAY to a great place to eat according to BOBBY. The traffic was light considering the time of day. ADRIANA checked out the sights and the people as they made their way through traffic. She was thrilled with the cities'excitement. BOBBY had been to NEW YORK CITY many times so he paid little attention to his surroundings.

They arrived along the harbor area. The small boats that took the people to the STATUE OF LIBERTY tours were plentiful. IT was a gorgeous day to be out on the sound. The limo had to be parked in a certain area and BOBBY and ADRIANA walked along with the thickened crowd. There seemed to be so much excitement in the air. Finaly they were now aboard enjoying the excitement of the ride. IT was a gorgeous summer day to be out on the water. She loved the boat ride and BOBBY liked it too although he had a lot on his mind about business prospects he managed a smile here and there. She knew when he was quiet that he was thinking about business which always was his priority. Thats' why he was rich because he spent most of his time thinking about making money.

They took a lot of pictures of THE STATUE OF LIBERTY. She loved being on the boat and crusing the sound. She just loved the feel of NEW YORK CITY. The boat ride lasted a while and then they headed for the shore. She was getting tired and hungry now. She told BOBBY it was time for lunch and of course he agreed. HE called his limo driver and in a short while the limo arrived. They headed back into the TRIBECCA AREA where BOBBY knew of some high class places to have lunch. She was so hungry she did not fuss about where they would eat. The limo arrived and they headed to TRIBECCA. She was pleased knowing they were going to a nice place to eat and BOBBY always had good taste when it came to eating out. HE loved elegant places too. They arrived at a lavious restaurant. The limo driver left them at the front door of the place. She was all excited for she had never been to this top notch place ever before. BOBBY handed the door man a twenty dollar bill as they entered the most beautiful place she had ever experienced.

They were seated on the viranda. IT was a beautiful day the sun shining so gorgeous and the warm breezes blowing off from the ocean just off the right side of the viranda. She just could not believe the beauty she was beholding. She was wondering what it cost for the average meal served here. BOBBY never worried about cost for after all he was a multi-millionaire. Money was never an issue. ADRIANA had money too but no where near what he was worth. She was far from broke. They were given menues and the waiter poured two glasses of spring water.

Within a short while they decded on what they'd have for lunch. BOBBY ordered two steaks with baked potatoes and each a salad. She was happy with their choices. The waiter brought their bottle of FRENCH WINE and poured them each a glass. They toasted their relationship as always. SO far it had been a wonderful day. IT was always a great day to be with BOBBY.

BOBBY reached into his suit jacket and produced a ring box. HE took her hand in his and told her to open the box while he got on one knee to ask her to marry him. She nearly fainted as she tried it on. IT fit perfect and she went speechless for a few minutes. She started to cry and said yes at least five times. BOBBY sat down once more leaned over the table and kissed her. She was still speechless.

BOBBY told her he had planned to ask her to marry him while they were in NEW YORK CITY. She was shaking with excitement. Now all they had to do was set a date and plan the wedding which no doubt would be like a fairytale wedding.

The waiter brought their food. The salad was placed first on the table, then the steaks and potatoes. Then the waiter refilled their wine glasses. They drank a toast to their engagement. They were truly in love. Now they ate and made small talk. She kept looking at her ring, tears filling her eyes with boundless happiness. BOBBY had sure surprised her. She never had any idea that this day would be the best day so far of her life.

She was on her way of becoming MRS. BOBBY EDWARDS. She was really a special person now. Every woman she knew would be envious for sure. She was now going to be treated like the first lady of the WHITE HOUSE. Lucky for her she was BOBBY EDWARDS'woman. She already had visions in her head of the most lavious wedding money could buy. BOBBY would spare no expenses for his bride.

After dinner they had more wine to drink. BOBBY phoned his limo driver and told him they'd be heading to ROCKERFELLA CENTER NBC to see the ROCKETTES presentation by five pm. ADRIANA was so surprised not expecting this show on top of a grand day already.

BOBBY sure surprised her. She was still shaken and overwhelmed. The limo pulled up to the front of the theater. The limo driver opened the doors and then left. There was only a short line awaiting entrance so the wait was short. The line moved quickly surprisingly. IN no time they were seated for the afternoon performance. ADRIANA was speechless from the excitement. BOBBY was glad he took her by surprise. HE loved this girl more than he ever loved anyone ever before. HE had never been this happy either. This was the best time in his life he thought.

After the show the limo driver picked them up and they were off to have dinner at any place she chose from her NEW YORK CITY brochures. ADRIANA could not believe the fantastic day she already had. She was so hyper that she could not think clear. She now chose a place and of course it was fine with BOBBY. Bobby would eat any kind of food so it did not matter to him at all where they ate and certainly high prices did not bother him at all. After all BOBBY EDWAEDS was a multimillionaire. HE was worth more than the CATHOLIC CHURCH he attended as a child. HIS mom had sent BOBBY and BLAKE to a strict CATHOLIC SCHOOL. But boys will be boys like the saying goes and they grew up agressive as well as rich and brash as can be. Why not after all they were the EDWARDS boys.

They found the place to eat in the heart of MANHATTAN. AS she stepped from the limo she gazed at the place she had chosen. She felt she picked out something they'd both enjoy. IT turned out to be a steak house. HE was impressed with her choice although she had randomly selected a top notch steak house and not knowing NEW YORK it surprised him a great deal. They were seated quickly and the waiter was very promote suggesting a nice dinner wine. BOBBY chose an expensive wine and the waiter hurried off to the wine cellar. IN a short time the waiter returned, poured the wine and took their dinner orders. They made small talk in the meantime discussing NEW YORK CITY and the day they had had already. The waiter brought their salads and coffee. Then came the biggest steaks ever. ADRIANA was surprised by the size of the steaks. BOBBY was impressed too.

BOBBY thanked her for picking out such an exclusive place. She smiled warmly by his kind words spoken. BOBBY knew he had a woman of substance now. HE sure picked the right one to hook up with for the rest of his life, unlike his dead brother BLAKE who had been married four times none of which worked out. Well BLAKES' choices were not always for the right reasons. The consequences for his actions proved fatal in the end. BLAKE had learned the hard way. HE could have had a different lifestyle after all he was super wealthy. Women were his downfall. HE also drank a lot. HE had bad relationships. HE'D spoil the women he dated to the extreme as long as they kept his sexual favors at their best. HE had a sexual appetite different than BOBBYS'. BLAKE was always looking for new ways to enjoy sex and he liked men as well as women in his sex games. HE had an undying hunger for fullfilling his fantasies. BOBBY was so different. BOBBY was crazy for women. Even in highschool he was a ladies' man.

Now BLAKE was part of the families' history. BOBBY was the super star of the family now. BOBBY felt bad the way BLAKE had died that day in the street by gun fire from a US MARSHAL. How tragic it seemed to him seeing his brother die by taking a bullet to end his middle aged brothers' life. Blake had the world by the ass if only he had been straight up with the law things would have worked out some other way. GOD how things worked out.

BOBBY now was the leader of a multimillion dollar company and still an icon in his own right. HE does not live in his dead brothers' shadow. HE is a man who stands heads above any others. HE is a well respected business man throuh out the world. Everyone knows the EDWARDS'name.

Now in the near future there was a large wedding to plan. The EDWARDS'family was going to get a daughter-in law and BOBBY was excited about taking a wife after being single so many years. Well the rest of the night went smooth. ON the way home they stopped at the local DAIRY QUEEN for some icecream and headed home. HE was exhausted and wanted a little relaxation in the sack with his future wife. She needed some tlc too. There was no saving herself for the honeymoon for she was well broken in. She was always in need of sex. IN a short time they were pulling into their driveway.

ADRIANA was thinking ahead about the wedding plans. She wanted a big wedding and BOBBY seemed okay at that after all he could well afford the best wedding of the century. AS they made their way up the stairs it started to rain. BOBBY unlocked the front door. She kicked her shoes off as BOBBY put on a few lights in the hall and living room. BOBBY went right to the bar and poured two glasses of the best FRENCH WINE. HE called for a toast to their future as well as the celebration of their engagement. BOBBY it seemed realized just what he had now. Their future was subject to change. Happiness now was theirs to behold. Now a wedding had to be planned. ADRIANA knew a lot of people and had numerous relatives, so did BOBBY so a real big wedding would work out fine.

She had a lot to plan now that the diamond was on her finger. This was going to be the wedding of the century. All she could think about is being MRS. BOBBY EDWARDS. She would be the envy of all her friends and GOD wait until she broke the news to her parents. HER parents had met BOBBY once when they were in L/A a while ago on vacation. They seemed to like BOBBY and he liked them too of course.

They knew their daughter would be very well provided for. Adriana was a lucky lady finding BOBBY EDWARDS. They had met in a night club a few years ago. HE spotted her from across the dance floor. They danced a few dances, had a few drinks, chatted somewhat and she went home with him. After a weekend spent at his place and hot sex he asked her to move in with him. She was shocked by all the attention. She was pleased he asked her. IN a few days she moved all her personal gear into his place.

She hired movers to move her gear. BOBBY was happy that she'd move in. This was a major move for her as well as for BOBBY. This meant there was a seriouness on their relationship. This was the ultimate thing to solidify their lives. ADRIANA had always dreamed of being married to BOBBY but now her dream was shaping into a reality. She was really excited after all BOBBY was a multimillionaire. HE could give her the world. HE loved her enough to shower her with whatever she wanted at any given point in time. After all she was to be MRS. BOBBY EDWARDS. She enjoyed being spoiled. BOBBY loved to spoil her anyway. BOBBY was so pleased with her. HE knew she was the right choice to be his wife. She was beautiful, smart, outgoing, athletic, and a great lover. She had it all. BOBBY had indeed found his soul mate. True happiness for both of them prevailed. A new start for a nice couple. ITwas a shame BOBBYS'parents had died years ago and of course his brother BLAKE was deceased too, but he had relatives and loads of friends and associates that would be invited to the biggest wedding of the century after all BOBBY was super rich and could afford the best of everything that was needed to have the grandest wedding of them all.

They had to spend some serious time getting ready for that special day. They no doubt would have a big church wedding. BOBBY was a CATHOLIC and so was ADRIANA. There was a real large cathederal in center of the city and BOBBY knew FATHER SATTANNI for years so no doubt they'd get married there. BOBBY had donated thousands of dollars over the years to his church. Father Sattanni had known BOBBY since he was a child and knew his brother BLAKE TOO, plus the priest knew his parents, a few aunts, a few uncles too. IT would certainly be a wedding to remember. IT would cost a fortune but to BOBBY it did not matter for money was not a problem ever to an EDWARDS' guy.

The next few days would be busy looking for a bakery for the wedding cake, invitations, and other preps to get this wedding off the ground. IT was going to be quite a challenge to get the prep work done. They were excited about planning the wedding of the year. IT would be spectacular for sure. The guest list would be quite extensive.

They sat down that evening and discussed the preliminary planning stages. There was so much to prep for. The excitement increased as thay talked further. GOD where was the point to really start at?There was so much to do to get ready for this wedding.

ADRIANA kept looking at her ring as though this was a dream and not a reality. She was virtualy walking on air. She could not wait to show everyone her diamond. The ring was rated over fiftheen carrots with fiftheen hand cut diamonds designed like a group of flowers. IT was exceptional. After all she was exceptional and she was going to be the bride of one of the richest men in the world. She was in the limelight for sure. The whole world would know her name and just who she was at this point in time. She'd be the envy of any woman on earth for sure. Being MRS. BOBBY EDWARDS gave her prestigeand dominance among the rich and the famous.

BOY she had come a long way in life to end up as MRS. BOBBY EDWARDS. Before she met him she use to follow articles in the finance newspapers about him as well as BLAKE his deceased brother. She was fascinated with the EDWARDS' family. She admired the rich and swore one day she'd be the bride of a very rich. HER dreams were becoming a reality. She had come from a above average family but was not wealthy like the EDWARDS'guys. IT would be tough to be as rich as THE EDWARDS for their old money went back in time to their great grandparents who were stock investors and had done well. She at this point felt vibrant, wealthy, spoiled etc. She felt like a princess in a fairytale living the life in luxury. She soon would be MRS. BOBBY EDWARDS so she was in the spotlight and soon would be in all the newspapers as well as well as the popular magazines. Everyone would envy ADRIANA. Everyone would know her face and her name. She had made it to the top. She was somebody special. She would soon be more popular than THE FIRST LADY. She was proud of who she was. She could stand proud for she soon would be MRS. BOBBY EDWARDS. The world would stand up and take notice of her and of course they already know of BOBBY EDWARDS. HE know doubt was just as well known as our president. After all he was one of a handfull of multimillionaires. HE owned the biggest soap company in the world. HE owned his own banks as well. HE had a few real rich friends as well.

Now they had a few more days to relax in NEW YORK CITY-then back to L/A to plan the biggest wedding ever. The next day they were going to sightsee more perhaps the EMPIRE STATE BUILDING. BOBBY knew his way around the city for he had been there many times but ADRIANA had not. This was her first trip to the eastcoast and it excited her. She fell in love with NEW YORK. She found the city to be invigorating. She liked it as much as CALIFORNIA. She was fascinated by the people and how crowded the streets were as they walked along admiring the skyscrapers towering to the sky. NEW YORK CITY made her feel alive. Everyday was an adventure. She loved the hustle and bustle of the city. BUT soon they had to head home to L/A and plan the grandest wedding ever there was.

The crowds thickened as the day turned into evening. People were running about hailing cabs, heading to dinner somewhere no doubt then out to a show on BROADWAY. This city was so alive with activity at all hours. ADRIANA adored NEW YORK. BOBBY was glad he took her there so she could see how crazy it was compared to L/A. BOBBY had a few favorite cities. HE loved NEW YORK, DALLAS, L/A and of course MIAMI as well. She had not traveled as much as he did after all he was the C.e.o. of a major corporation in AMERICA.

They had a few more days in the city then would head home to L/A. They loved NEW YORK CITY but he had his corporate office in L/A so business had to be taken care of although he had real good people working for him when he was gone. Plus she wanted to get started on the wedding planning. The sooner the better. NO date was set yet but that would be worked out. After all ADRIANA never worked for BOBBY took care of her. Money was never a problem.

Several days passed. They were now at JFK AIRPORTclearing security. IT was time almost for their flight home to L/A. They were anxious to get home. The next few weeks would be the planning stages of the wedding. Plus BOBBY had some important buying decisions in regards to his company. Things now were going to be hectic for a while. Now that they cleared security they were allowed to board the aircraft. IN a matter of an hour they were in the air heading home to the sunshine state. There was so much to be done. BOBBY had to return today for tomorrow there was a board meeting slated for nine a/m. The flight time was about five hours.

After what seemed like a few hours the plane was landing at L. A. X. BOBBY grabbed a few small bags and ADRIANA did like wise. They were down at the luggage area in a short time awaiting their suitcases. HE called his limo driver who arrived in a short while. OFF they went quickly heading for his mansion. BOBBY felt satisfied that they were home at last. There was no place like home at least to him that is. Traffic wasn't bad as they headed onto THE PACIFIC COAST HIGHWAYwest towards BOBBYS' place.

Finaly they reached BOBBYS' driveway and pulled in front of the spacious southern styled mansion. BOBBYS' six staff members greeted them at the door. BOBBY helped his fiance out of the limo for she had taken a nap on the way home and was a little drowsy.

BOBBY helped ADRIANA reach the couch. She laid there for a while closing her eyes trying to shut the rest of the world out at least for a brief moment. She had jet lag for sure. She slept quietly while BOBBY caught up with his staff who gave an account briefly to bring BOBBY up to date. BOBBY was pleased with the latest news from his employees for everything seemed to be in good order. BOBBY had a seasoned staff who were just wonderful and did their jobs well. BOBBY lit a cigarette as he fiddled with his piles of mail.

BOBBY sorted his mail seperating business from personal ones. HE was overwhelmed by the stacks of mail on his coffee table. HE had multiple business contacts. There was so much mail relative to his soap company too. HE spent millions in advertising also so as to keep a competitive position. His company was the number one soap company in the country. His grandparents had established the company so most of the money was what they called old money handed down to his parents, then his brother, then to him of course. NO matter what he was super rich.

BOBBY took his mail to his office on the lower floor to award him privacy at least for a while as he gathered his thoughts as well as he sifted through the heap of mail. AT his office in L/A his secretary took care of the mail sorting it down and fed him the most important stuff. Plus he was at the office long hours deep into the night going over mail, e-mails, packages among other sorts that needed his attention. IT was tough being a C.e.o. of a major corporation. HE had a company of over five hundred employees not counting those that labored in the factory making soap daily. HE worked hard to hold that number one soap company position.

BLAKE his deceased brother ran the company a lot different but now BOBBY being the head of the company ran things so much better for he was on top of the day operations. HE was a middle aged man with numerous ambitions. There was no one who had his drive. HE was on top of his game. HE was quite a business man. Working hard all the time.

ADRIANA made a pot of coffee and sat for a while on the patio enjoying the warm breezes from off the ocean. She lit a cigarette and tried to unwind. What she needed was some hot sex to loosen her up some. Sex always relaxed her. She'd have to wait a while BOBBY was deeply involved with business matters at the moment. She could understand how business took priority. She lit a second cigarette. HER pussy was getting hotter by the moment and soon BOBBY better pleasure her or she'd have to pleasure herself on the waterbed with her vibrator. IT was not unusual for her to wet her vibrator with a fluid then insert it deep into her vagina. She could get partialy off and have BOBBY finish her off later. She was a hot mama with many sexual needs to be satisfied.

ADRIANA with help from the kitchen staff got supper prepared. They were celebrating with steaks, baked potatoes, salads of all sorts. BOBBY would announce the biggest wedding plans of the year. HIS staff would be shocked. NO one had any idea that BOBBY was going to be married. His staff knew about ADRIANA of course for BOBBY had been with her a long time but, the staff knew hc was a ladies' man prior with his variety of women that came into his life. Women were a commodity with him. Adriana had won his heartand he realized she was the right choice to marry him. They would be the most famous couple in the world once they tied the knot.

Finaly BOBBY finished sorting his mail. IT was close to nine p/m time to have one of those DELMONICO STEAKS. HE headed up the stairs to the elaborate dining room. Adriana smiled at him as he sat next to her. The meal was served. BOBBY was famished. BY the time they finished eating it was close to eleven p/m. ADRIANA was ready for bed. She was horny and BOBBY had a free day tomorrow so they could have lots of sex with no hesitation. She glanced at him that certain way that was a written invitation in a sense to get to bed early as they could for she could not wait to much longer. HE got her message as she rubbed her foot up onto his leg under the table. HE took her by the hand and they headed for the master bedroom. She was hot to the touch. They closed their bedroom door. She undressed quickly throwing her clothes onto the red leather chair. She hopped onto the waterbed, her legs spread eagle. She was ready. BOBBY joined her. IN a flash he was inside her pumping her as hard and as fast as he could. She had multiple climaxes causing her to gyrate her body like a woman gone completely mad making her lose touch with reality.

She was turned on and it would be a while before she could turn off. BOBBY knew how to satisfy her and took his time doing so. This sex session no doubt would last all night. She loved every minute of the love and affection.

The next morning BOBBY had an important phone call from his office. HE had some important people who had called who wanted to meet with him in regards to a sale worth millions of dollars to him. HE had sent a bid out on a small soap company and they accepted his offer. BOBBY set up a time with his secretary and hung up. HE showered and ate a quick breakfast and hurried out the door while ADRIANA slept late. After all this was a major buy out that he could not miss out on. HE had wanted that company for quite sometime now. Here it was up for grabs. HE had to move on this deal and right away. Buying out this company would make his company the international leader in the soap business with very little competition. His company would control 98%of the soap sales in the entire world. BOBBY wanted that position.

Meanwhile at home ADRIANA was creating a list of wedding plans. GOD she thought there was so much to do and her and BOBBY needed a date yet. They would discuss that as soon as soon as he had a day off when he was not under the pressure of business. She understood that business came first after all it kept both of them in a luxury living lifestyle. BOBBY would come through for her no doubt. This marriage was a real big step for him after all he never was married before unlike BLAKE his brother who had had four wives. BLAKE collected women like other guys collect baseball cards. They had no sentimental value, just lust, hot sex and murder. After that their purpose had been served. BLAKE was somewhat a serial killer in a sense. HE married for all the wrong reasons. BOBBY was so different, so decent, so straight up, so honest. ADRIANA had gotten the best guy that was still single. IT was her fate to marry BOBBY EDWARDS and she was getting nervous waiting for the big day.

When he returned home they'd talk some more for she wanted to make wedding plans. She was excited to say the least. She heard a car drive up and sure it was BOBBY returning. She was glad he was home. After he relaxed she would bring up the wedding plans. She met him at the door with a quick kiss. HE seemed to be in a good mood. She guessed he had closed the deal. BOBBY shared the good news with her. The new company he bought cost a few million. HE was pleased with the purchase. She was happy for him. She put on a pot of coffee. BOBBY lit a cigarette trying to relax. She wanted to bring up creating a date for their wedding but was not sure where to start.

BOBBY lit another cigarette. She poured two coffees and sat down next to him. She smiled warmly at him, he smiled back at her. HE now broke the silence with a question about the wedding date planning. Neither one of them had any date in mind. BOBBYS' business took priority. They needed time to plan out the date as well as the numerous things that were needed to solidify the wedding. There was so much to plan and put in place for the biggest day in their lives.

She asked BOBBY what month and date would not conflict with his business but he was not sure due to the way business was going. HE promised her by the upcoming weekend he'd have an answer for her. She smiled and he smiled backthen bent to kiss her gently. She knew he would keep his word. BOBBY never lied to her, nor ever did he disappoint her in any way either. A few days passed and he took a day off and they used that day to do some planning for their wedding. GOD where to start was the question. With a pen and a legal pad they sat at the kitchen table putting ideas of how to go about this wedding. This was not going to be a simple task at all after all he had family, she had family, friends were plentiful, business associates of BOBBYS' were to numerous to even start to count. This was going to be a project alright. They sat there for hours going over ideas. BY now the ash tray was fullof cigarette butts, the coffee had grown cold, but still they continued.

She wanted a break so pushed back her chair, lit a cigarette, smiled briefly at BOBBY and finaly kissed him on his forehead. BOBBY also needed a break. HE lit a cigar and got up and stretched some. They had written many ideas and needed a few minutes to break away.

This wedding was going to be spectacular to say the least. They would be more famous than the president and his wife. They took a break from their planning as the phone rang. They let the call go to voicemail. They both lit a cigarette and tried to relax. She poured two glasses of FRENCH WINE. They toasted to their wedding plans and their future. The phone rang again this time BOBBY answered the call. His secretary called him to notify him that his next stock meeting was coming up next week. HE chatted with her for a few minutes as he scribbled the message on his legal pad. Then he hung up the phone and sipped at his expensive wine. BOBBY loved imported expensive wines.

Adriana got up and walked onto the patio briefly. The sun was going down and a nice breeze caressed her face. She smiled to herself and walked back into the kitchen. HE was still sitting there but seemed content with how their day was going. They needed a master plan to put in place. Their wedding no doubt would cost nearly a million dollars or so after all ADRIANA was his princess and deserved the greatest wedding of the century.

BOBBY poured two more glasses of wine. IT was nearly supper time. BOBBYS' personal cook attended to their supper needs. BOBBY had a staff of six at his beach house in MALIBU. They would have supper on the patio tonight.

ADRIANA sat on the deck smoking her cigarette, listening to her portable radio. She loved classical music. The warm air relaxed her as she sipped her wine. BOBBY joined her. They were content that they started their wedding plans. NO date had been set yet. The servents brought their food out to the patio tables. The sun now had gone down and there was a nice breeze off the ocean. They ate while making small talk, mostly about the weather. After dinner they each had a cigarette along with more wine. Adriana was getting horny. She needed some hot sex to relax her. She hinted to BOBBY about a quicky. BOBBY was ready it seemed also. They walked hand in hand to the master bedroom closing the door behind them and locking it.

She undressed quickly. HE already was getting a solid erection. They were into position in no time. HE was gentle as he put his penis inside her as she spread her legs real wide. HE rubbed her thighs and sucked her hardened nipples bringing her to a orgasm quickly. She gyrated her legs taking him deeper inside her making groaning sighs as she did so. HE could not hold his sperm back to much longer. HE asked her if she was ready to come which she agreed upon. HE had finaly ejaculated inside her making her blush and yell for more. HE smothered her with kisses. Finaly they broke loose. They both reached for their cigarettes. IT was the time to relax as the sweat poured off their bodies.

They started talking about the wedding. There was an all glass church nearby that would suffice and would hold a number of patrons. BOBBY wanted the best wedding ever.

HE was wealthy and could afford it. HE also wanted the best for ADRIANA. They had a long talk about how to get certain things ready for the big day. There were so many things to finalize.

They had sex again this time taking her over the edge in her orgasms. They now were both exhausted and he faced a busy day the next morning it was time to call it a day. She cuddled up next to him and was asleep in no time. HE gazed at her beautiful body wanting her again but there was no way that would happen for he met the point of sheer exhaustion. HE covered her up with the comforter and kissed her on her forehead. HE shut off the lamp and laid there for a few minutes thinking soon she'd be MRS. BOBBY EDWARDS. They had come a long way within their relationship. HE thought GOD I will no longer be a single guy. I will be the husband of a beautiful woman.

The alarm clock went off waking BOBBY right away. HE had to shower, have breakfast and be on his way by nine a/m. HE had a busy day planned, with several meetings, etc. HE showered, made his coffee, dressed in one of his best suits, ate a muffin, sipped coffee and was well on his way out the door heading to the world of business as usual.

HE took the black MERCEDES. HE headed out to the main highway south of his location. IT was a balmy day and the a/c kept him comfortable. HE had to face a tough day at meetings and whatever the day brought along.

When he arrived at his office the place was extremely busy. HE had his first meeting to begin with in a few minutes. The boardroom was crowded with all his dignitaries. They were there to discuss the purchase of the small company he had bid on recently. The meeting ran into overtime. Three hours later it finaly was over. HE stepped away and called ADRIANA. HE told he'd run late tonight for supper. She was not surprised. HE apologized. HE returned to his office where he was meeting with a doctor friend of his. They were meeting to discuss a clinic to be built there at his office. IT was going to cost a few million but BOBBY felt that his employees should have something in place. HEwanted to show he appreciated his employees. IT was not about money at all but caring for his employees. BLAKE his brother never did anything for his employees when he ran the company. BOBBY was different, had compassion not like BLAKE. HE wanted to show he was humanistic. They talked about the projectfor an hour or so. The new building will start to be built the following spring. This was the agreement to get it under construction. IT was one of the important contracts on BOBBYS' agenda. They parted company and BOBBY went on with his day. The day was full with more meetings and four o'clock was a long way off.

BOBBY was getting tired. The day moved along nicely though. When four o'clock arrived he could not wait to get out of there. HE called his limo driver to get him home leaving the MERCEDES to be serviced.

The limo arrived and off it headed to the house in MALIBU. The sun was going down and a gentle breeze was blowing. The limo driver had the a/c going for his employer. The ride home took almost an hour due to the five o'clock traffic at this point in time. BOBBY opened his laptop and reviewed his daily notes. AS they pulled into BOBBYS' driveway. ADRIANA waved from the window and ran to the door to greet BOBBY. The limo driver parked the car and went direct to his quarters. IT was now six fifteen and ADRIANA had the cook grill a few steaks., make a salad, and fries for their supper. Also she poured two chilled glasses of wine for her and BOBBY.

The small bits of conversation turned into quite a bit of plans for the wedding. BOBBY had already reserved the all glass church and its'oversized dining room, a reception room that overlooked the PACIFIC OCEAN. She was pleased to hear that bit of news. The wedding cake was to be ordered shortly based on the date of marriage which had not been decided yet. They talked for hours and took several notes on decisive issues. Several things were taken care of now. BOBBY poured two more glasses of wine. The talk continued.

The next morning was SATURDAY at last a free day for BOBBY with the company closed on weekends was a good thing. HE could relax all day. They could plan more of the wedding. Adriana was still asleep as BOBBY popped open his laptop. HE went over his e-mails which at times were hundreds still waiting to be reviewed. IT was a lot of work but he would review only the important items. She awoke around eleven a/m. HE fussed about and made her breakfast. After she ate she went back to bed hoping he'd want a quickie. BOBBY was caught up in his e-mails and had to respond to many affecting his business. HE was doing well but there were sacrifices to be had when it came down to the business itself took priority of course. BOBBY took his time scruitinizing his e-mails and ADRIANA fell asleep now so the house was quiet as a closed church.

BOBBY sat for hours working on his e-mails. Some he deleted quickly. Finaly he was tired of this and felt guilty not working on his wedding plans. HE grabbed his yellow pad and reread the old notes first trying to get more ideas. The wedding date itself still undecided but had to be set up soon. HE sat there sipping his wine and now lit a cigarette. ADRIANA staggered sleepily to the kitchen. She slipped her arms around him, her naked body caressing his back, her breasts soft to his touch as he reached around her grabbing her gently trying to kiss her hardened nipples. IN seconds he carried her to the bedroom and in no time he was inside her pounding away at her hot flesh, her pussy wet with desire. She gyrated her body like an animal in heat, yelling and moaning wanting him deeper inside of her. She climaxed real hard and had multiple orgasms driving her out of reality into a world of sexual desire where an orgasm was a winner. BOBBY was holding back waiting for that moment of release. She caressed his balls and that triggered his sperm to flow like a torrent river of desire.

HE filled her crevice making her even more hot with desire. She was wet between her legs and his cock slipped out of her for a moment.

BOBBY needed a breather for a few minutes, his body a pouring sweat now. She could wear him down. HE loved her but GOD at times she could expect more than he could satisfy her with. HE reached for his cigarettes lit two—gave her one. She got up and poured two glasses of wine from the cooler behind the bar. She smiled warmly as he eyed her large breasts. She sat there on the edge of the bed with her legs spread as wide as can be giving him a great look at her hairy pussy which was still hot with desire. What a night it had been. She was sweating and turned on the a/c. BOBBY sipped his chilled wine as he admired her naked body. HE wanted to take her on again but the desire was there but the energy was depleted. HE needed to rest before continuing on. She was full of energy as though she caught a second breath already.

The next few weeks seemed to fly by quickly. ADRIANA and BOBBY buckled down and got more serious about the wedding plans. ITwas decided they would marry the following JUNE. IT seemed so far off but time sometimes moves fast.

IT took some doing to get everything in place but after many weeks of planning the deal was done. NOW it was wait on the calendar months as they passed by. BOBBY figured use his own limo to get them to the church. HIS driver is familiar with the area. Plus why pay for another limo when he owns his own. ITwas now a matter of time. AT least the first plans were set up.

The next day was SUNDAY and BOBBY layed around all morning. HE watched the news as ADRIANA slept late. HIS merger with ALLIED SOAP COMPANY made the headlines. IT was just a matter of time and he'd control 100%of the soap industry which was worth millions of dollars. BOBBY smiled to himself knowing that deaLclosed. What was the next business deal?BOBBY was on top in investing money in the stock market. HE had done well so far and his company was on FORBES 'lists for months. HE knew how to place money in the volitile market place. HE lit a cigarette and poured himself glass of wine. HE celebrated alone his big success story. Finaly ADRIANA was behind him with opened arms and a naked body any man would die for. HE turned around and picked her up headed straight for the waterbed seeking action. She was hot to the touch, ready, willing and able. HE placed her gently on the cool waterbed and in seconds was inside her. HE had no problem keeping up with her. She had moves that would make a dead man come. She gyrated her torso almost to the point of losing touch with reality. She loved sex more than anything on this mans'earth. She was dam good at it too. They made love for quite some time and then rested lighting a cigarette to relax. She had given him a hell of a workout. She satisfied BOBBY never disappointing him ever. They now drank a toast to their upcoming marriage

TN so many months they would be MR. andMRS. BOBBY EDWARDS. Time seemed to be passing by at a fast pace. She headed for the masterbath room. She stepped into the shower grabbing her soap and washcloth. She was full of sweat anxious to rinse off in cold water which stimulated her. Then the shower door opened and there he stood ready to take her on again in another sex session. HE moved closer to her and in moments lifted her in the air and placed his penis inside her. She yelled out loud as he pushed her gently against the wall as the cold water covered their bodies. She was hot all over again as he shot his load of sperm inside her. She went psycho on him gyrating like an animal truly out of control losing reality. HE broke free of her as the cold water caused him cold chills making him shakey even though he was giving his best shot to keep going as best he could but the cold water stunned him into reality. HE apologized to her. She kissed him gently. They left the shower and headed to the large cool waterbed. They were both exhausted but relaxed now. She smiled then lit a cigarette. BOBBY left the room then returned with two chilled glasses of imported wine. They again toasted to their future marriage.

THE next morning BOBBY had to head to the office. There were meetings planned, lunch with other company c.e.o. s' to discuss possible mergers or buyouts. IT was all about money today. BOBBY was a little nervous his confidence shaken somewhat. He hated MONDAYS for they were upsetting to him. However he'd get through no doubt at all. HE took a deep breath as he entered the board room. There they sat the twelve deciples as he called them. They could make or break his day. HE just wanted to get this meeting over with. IT was an hour of nothing but questions and tough answers. HE showed confidence as he reached the podium. The directors were not short of tyrany for they wanted to know how much more money he was going to spend to enhance the largest soap company in the world. They wanted answers and wanted them now. BOBBY showed a flair of arrogance at this point making the entire board members quiet down and stay quiet.

BOBBY was in no mood for bullshit. Finaly the bewitching hour passed and it was brought to a close. BOBBY moved on to what was next on the agenda. HIS cell phone rang and he answered it because it was ADRIANA. They chatted briefly. Then BOBBY had to attend another meeting. MONDAYS were a bitch for him. HE had no choice for he was c.e.o. and that was his responsibility. IT was close to noon when his next meeting had ended.

Meanwhile ADRIANA got a call from the bridal gown store. The custom gown she ordered was ready for pickup or delivery. She told the lady to have it sent to the MALIBU address. Within an hour the gown arrived. ADRIANA was pleased with her purchase. She looked the gown over smiling to herself. She loved the hand sewn pearls and the laces were gorgeous. She covered the gown in plastic and set it in the walk in closet. She only had six months to go to wear it and already she was excited. She could not wait to tell BOBBY it arrived. HE had not seen the dress yet but soon enough the big day would arrive and he would be amazed by its'beautyfor sure.

IT was nearly four p/m when BOBBY finished up his day. IT had been hectic and he just wanted to get home. HE dialed his cell phone for his limo driver for he was to tired to drive home in traffic for at least another hour. The limo pulled up in front of his office building just as BOBBY came out the front door of the all glass framed building. AT last his business day had ended.

BOBBY climbed into the rear seat of the limo, lit a cigarette and dialed ADRIANAS' cell number. She picked up on the second ring. HE told her he was on his way home. She told him she loved him and hung up the phone. She ordered the servents to attend to the supper needs. ITwas nearly six p/m when she heard the limo pull up into the circular driveway. She went to the door to greet BOBBY which was routine with her. She reached out for him and gave him a warm kiss as she held the screen door open. BOBBY was glad to be home. HE put down his computer case and his attache case and lit a cigarette while she poured two chilled glasses of wine for them.

IT had been a long day for BOBBY. The cook announced supper was ready on the patio deck. They walked hand in hand to the patio deck where the smell of the steaks got their attention. A nice salad also had been prepared. They made small talk and she told him about the wedding gown being delivered. HE seemed pleased. The servents served wine for both of them. The night breeze set its'warmth aglow across the patio. IT was a perfect summer night in MALIBU. A perfect night to dine out on the patio. The evening just was so special for the two lovers.

Months went by and suddenly it was JUNE 28TH their wedding date. ADRIANA was up super early and with the help of her maid she dressed into her beautiful pearl covered gown. She had about two hours to get ready to leave for the church. The limo was already there in the driveway polished and ready to roll. BOBBY would be driving himself in his black MERCEDES. HE did not want to see ADRIANA until she was standing at the altar. HE was real nervous as he paced the driveway smoking one cigarette after the other. AS time progressed he left for the church with his best man RON a former C.e.o. of his old company from years back. AS they drove along BOBBY smoked heavily nervous as anything. The ride to the church was about fourty five minutes. They arrived in plenty of time. The best man parked the car and lit a cigarette. They were at least an hour early. BOBBY was so nervous.

They could see all the cars in the church yard. BOBBYS' guest list was about five hundred people. The more BOBBY thought about the guests the more nervous he got. IN the meantime ADRIANA was on her way to the church. The limo cruised along at sixty with very little traffic. IN no time it seemed they were pulling into the church yard. BOBBY was already at the altar. The limo driver stopped at the church steps so ADRIANA and SUE her maid of honor could get out of the car. The organist was playing the wedding march as ADRIANAS' dad joined her to escort her down the aisle. ADRIANA was nervous. HER dad tapped her arm and smiled giving her confidence. The church pews were full of wedding guests, everyone waiting to see the beautiful bride arrive. BOBBY was standing nervously at the altar. ADRIANA walked with her dad calmly down the aisle smiling at everyone while cameras flashed endlessly at her. She was a vision of pure beauty. She now stopped in front of the priest. The priest went through the ritual marriage ceremony rights. IN a short while they were announced as husband and wife.

They kissed for the first time as husband and wife. NOW they went outside to take photos with their guests. IT was eighty five degrees even in the shade of the palm trees. After an hour of picture taking everyone entered the church hall for the reception. The hall was crowded as large as it was. There was close to five hundred guests all trying to get a close look at the newlyweds. Dinner was starting to be served as the band played popular songs. The bride and groom greeted passing guests. IT was hectic trying to keep with more photo taking by a professional photographer BOBBY had hired. After dinner the bride and groom opened gifts which was a endless mound of paper and boxes. They were thrilled by the beautiful gifts received. The reception lasted until eight p/m. Finaly the last guest was gone and BOBBY and ADRIANA now toasted their marriage with gleaming smiles.

IT had been the most wonderful day of their lives. BOBBYS' servents packed the gifts into BOBBYS' truck out behind the church. BOBBY and ADRIANA would now head home, change clothes, rest a while then would be driven to LAX AIRPORT to board their flight to JAMAICA. THEY'D be gone for two weeks for a well deserved honeymoon. BOBBY was glad he had time to relax and escape the world of business. ADRIANA was looking forward to swimming and boating on the island. She loved to travel and have never been out of the U. S. ever before. She was super excited. BOBBY was too looking forward to scuba diving and fishing of course which he loved.

They arrived home within an hour. BOBBY had the servants place the gifts in the guest bedroom for safe keeping. The wedding had been had went beautifuly and now they looked forward to a two week recuperation from the stress of all the festivities. ITwas great going away. They wanted away from L/A for a while. ITwas after nine p/m and they would be leaving for the airport soon. The limo pulled up into the driveway and LEO BOBBYS' driver opened the rear door. Two chilled glasses of wine awaited the newlyweds as LEO closed the door. LEO put on the a/c as he pulled out of the driveway. NOW it was off to the airport. BOBBY lit a cigarette and leaned back on his leather seat admiring his bride now dressed in a white blouse and white slacks and white sandals. She was still a vision of beauty. HE was dressed in a blue blazer, white shirt, white slacks and white tennis shoes. HE had on a white captains'hat on too.

The traffic was heavy as they entered the thruway. LEO kept a close eye on the traffic mounting on all sides. They arrived at the airport in plenty of time LEO helped the skycap load the bags onto a cart and wished the couple a great time and was gone in a flash. The couple passed through security and boarded the plane. IN a short while they were on their way to the islands of paradise. The captain announced the flight schedule. IN moments the plane was in the air. BOBBY looked out the window as the plane took off. The stewardess took their cart down the aisles serving drinks as the plane climbed higher into the clouds.

BOBBY and ADRIANA drank a toast to their lives for they were now MR. AND MRS. BOBBY EDWARDS. BOBBY leaned close to his bride kissing her softly. She smiled warmly as the plane reached a new height.

IN a few hours they would be landing in JAMAICA. ITwas two weeks of relaxation for the newlyweds. A well desrved break from the world of business. BOBBY ordered two more glasses of wine and again they toasted their special day. A few hours passed as it was dinner time now. The couple kissed again their hearts full of happiness. MR. AND MRS. BOBBY EDWARDS looked forward to the future.

THE END